Of Beasts & Beings

IAN HOLDING

SIMON &
SCHUSTER

London · New York · Sydney · Toronto

A CBS COMPANY

First published in Great Britain by Simon & Schuster UK Ltd, 2010
A CBS COMPANY

1 3 5 7 9 10 8 6 4 2

Simon & Schuster UK Ltd
1st Floor
222 Gray's Inn Road
London WC1X 8HB

www.simonandschuster.co.uk

Simon & Schuster Australia
Sydney

A CIP catalogue record for this book
is available from the British Library

ISBN: 978-1-84737-823-1

Typeset by M Rules
Printed in the UK by CPI Mackays, Chatham ME5 8TD

Praise for *Unfeeling*

'Rem... a kind of na... *Sund*

'One... *New*

'The... e of its own... *Tatle*

'Con... or and fear... lihood they... *Big I.*

'Fine... prose' *Guar*

'Deli... olonial whit... ity de-hum... es that both believe they were born to inherit' *The Leeds Guide*

'Surefooted prose gives this novel a devastating punch . . . a commanding picture of the land and nature as the ultimate power' *Metro*

'Brave and compelling'
Northern Advocate

'Narrated in spare, unfaltering prose, the novel is freighted with a profound sense of foreboding . . . Deftly builds a compelling story of a paradise lost'
Courier Mail

'A visceral and compelling narrative about murder, racism and vengeance'
Edmonton Journal

'Wonderful . . . The book is so brilliantly constructed and well written that I couldn't put it down. The story is harrowing, but not without humour, and the descriptions of the countryside are beautiful'
Globe and Mail

'A chilling and suspenseful story with a surprise twist. You will be kept engaged, especially in the shifting time spaces that Ian Holding writes so brilliantly'
Vancouver Sun

'A book I couldn't put down until the last screaming detail and whiplash surprise . . . Such a complete, double-sided vision of Africa it practically sings its passionate love while documenting horrors I hope I can forget someday. For a reader who wants to understand Africa, the real, complex Africa, this book has it all. And that's just one of its pluses – as a first novel, this is a terrifying joy'
Novelworld

Man is the most formidable of all the beasts and the only one that preys systematically on its own species.

William James,
Remarks at the Peace Banquet, 1904

1

He is taken captive on the outskirts of the city. He's picking among the ruins for food when they take him unawares on this hot gauzy morning. The sun tracks his seizure from above; he is a speck in the sweep of desolation about him. He had just come across the miracle of an unscathed vegetable patch studded with cabbages and beets and pumpkin and the bulbs of some sweet potatoes buried down hard in the ground. His mind is lost in an uncoiling rush of relief, his tongue and mouth unclotting. It is only a small vegetable patch. It's someone's sacred prize, their last oasis. Hemmed in with tall walls of bush and the skeletal stubs of hacked trees. He is busy gnawing at the stalks of the beets when a rope lassoes him taut around the throat. His breath is lost to an instant panic; he staggers on his feet but does not fall. A moment of blind senselessness overtakes him and then he glimpses the posed attitudes of three men brandishing machetes. They gather in, surround him. Their feet dig firm to the sod, their hands grip the rope as if taking part in a tug of war. He doesn't try to fight or flee.

One of them shouts something but he cannot understand what. Something crude and direct. He does not comprehend anything they say. His tongue is locked somewhere down his throat, his breath constricted by the snare staving into his vertebrae. A firm pair of hands clamp him by the neck and a foul stinking rag is stuffed into his mouth like a muzzle. Ragged and ropy, it smells of filth baked crisp in the sun. Or something fetid, something scum-like. Then the deeper odour of fear spikes his nostrils and a rapid swell slops up from his stomach. He stumbles about, moaning, shaking his head, but the harness they have him by is unyielding. He panics, sensing he is going to heave and choke, be overwhelmed from the inside out. The ground and the sky and the haggling bodies rove jaggedly, fusing in an odd cabal against which his actions are futile. He tries a feeble kick, to draw from inside himself and surge against them. Too little too late. They have him tight now, tighter.

They lead him off without a further word. His stomach is crouching in his throat; his wide eyes are burning. They lead him through the charred fields and the smoking debris of a shanty town recently levelled to the ground. He has to pick his way over a mangled pile of corrugated tin and shattered asbestos roofing as if dodging jetsam on a riverbank. The shards are sharp underfoot and stabs of spiky pain jerk up his shins. The shells of a few brick hovels stand here and there but the mud huts have been returned to the earth in an incendiary slew and the thatching lies thick in the black-yellow ash.

It hasn't rained for some time. Frayed canvas tarps are draped amongst the ruins and the air is thick with the smell of burnt plastic sheeting, the reeking tar of blistered tyres. They pass a creosote-stained wood shack with rows of pit latrines that have been bombed. The ruptured sewers snake in dark, wet runnels and lie drying in caked crusts of shit-soaked earth. The sick and emaciated were here not long ago. The pot-bellied, balding children, the grown-ups squatting on the ground gripping their cramped stomachs.

Now the smell is stiff and sits in his nose beyond the gag like an elastic fume. Between everything a sporadic spread of tin pots and utensils has been unearthed and scattered. Upturned stools and old bits of bedding with coils of springs are jutting out like disused antennae. This is all that escaped the torching and the advancing rampages of the horde, barbarians at some ancient bloodletting coasting on the shanties.

They march him on. As they veer round a cluster of shelled shacks they see the bodies of a family lying roasted on the ground, composed in a kind of petrified flux. The flares have pulled the skin tight across the faces and the whiteness of the teeth glints like slits of plastic or polyester grinning up at the smashed world. They pass on. The men don't comment or exclaim or bemoan. These fallen dead may have been members of the opposition or a household loyal to some rival faction. This is just a sight thrown up from a newly adjusted reality, a commonplace thing.

Their mismatched combat fatigues signals them out. Stalking effigies of violence, intimidation, fear. They may be from various factions of the militia. They may be offshoots of the army, the police, the opposition – on the rampage for anything they can loot or plunder or hijack. They wear camouflaged trousers in an array of mottled shades as if they have attempted to band together but the rest of their attire is indistinct: a frayed cotton shirt embossed with florid insignia; a grubby white vest torn at the side; a bare black chest muscled and sleeked with sweat. Their footgear is random too: a pair of dark leather boots, a pair of worn track shoes, a pair of old slops fixed over with wire gnarled around the toes. They have tied bandanas to their heads but with no legend or flag or colours of this side or that. In some ways they look like a comic trio out of a travelling circus, these teenagers rampaging as men.

On they lead him. Out of the spill of the shanty town and across a dead vlei burnt black and still sighing a wisp of smoke akin to the morning mist across the lowveld lands he may have come from. Or may not have. He has little clear memory of anything. He walks uneasily, fearing his feet will scorch. But they don't: the ash lies thick, a carpet of silken blackness into which the field now seeps. Nothing moves in this vacant rink but themselves and the rising smoke. On the turf there are bodies lying across the spiked scrub, rutted slits on their backs from the machete strikes and gobs of flesh scalloped from their buttocks.

They continue onwards and all the while he thinks of precious little beyond the discomfort of the gag and a faint pulsing alarm at his predicament. He thinks of the vegetables left bedded in their neat, prim rows. He had come so close to their sweet pleasures. He had sensed them and sniffed them out and been brought to them perhaps by some act of providence. They were his for the taking. He had found them and for those moments he owned them. There in that theatre of chaos he had stood relishing such gifts before his luck ran out.

They may have stumbled upon him by chance, out scouting for opportunities. What luck for them. Their brutal strength, the rope their weapon. Or they may have knelt in the scrub waiting for his hunger to send him creeping from the barren bushes. Like a fisher in his skiff, lobbing baited hooks to the dark reedy pool, hooking him in their creel. This small victory would always be theirs. A small battle they had won in a war that was too big for them.

It's bizarre to think they didn't plunder the vegetables before him. That they weren't sat there on the ruffed sod with that blanking ecstasy drawn across their tear-stained faces, the relief, the joy, clawing at the bulbs and tubers and leaves as he was. There must be some ill-gotten source that keeps them fed in these desperate days of famine. The dry ashen lands, the unyielding skies. The fertilizer rotten. The pumps rusted, stripped to the core and the water pipes ripped whole from the ground a long time ago. There must be something that keeps their stomachs full and their minds ticking and allows them to plot their treachery. Some strange devil's bedfellows they must be.

Until they approach the main highway leading directly into the city he plods along in their grasp diffidently enough, as if time itself has muffled his mind against the blows of the heat and the carnage. Now, though, he begins to tense. He senses the danger of walking a path travelled by every bandit and his brother. He knows to avoid the sight of roads. When stumbling on a stretch of asphalt he has always stopped and turned round and slunk off. Here, they are poised to encounter one faction of militia or the other, intent on guarding the entry and exit of the city for their own travails, as if they were savage trolls at a sentry posting. He begins to strain against the rope. He feels it tighten at his throat and his eyes widen. The man leading him shouts *Ewe!* and yanks on the rope and shoots him a threatening glance. On they pull him.

The road is deserted of all traffic save the occasional sweep of jeeps that thunder by, laden with men shouting victory songs and waving their AK47s in some futile celebration. The jeeps are military, though other factions drive similar ones. After several convoys pass without incident, his mood eases and he walks on again. No one will stop them and ask questions of the militia who have taken him hostage and are leading him off with a rope bundled round him and a gag in his mouth. There will be no spate of fighting in the midst of which he may be able to wrestle and break free. The jeeps drive on past their ambling band and it is possible they may not even see him. If they do then they obviously don't care a passing moment for his plight, such is the new order here flexing its iniquitous brawn. So much for that.

The battery of convoys come and go and the road is lined with the carcasses of burnt-out cars heaped here and there. No one else strolls about. They approach the forlorn grey city. Even from a distance it exudes a clouding eeriness. When they reach the outer suburbs there is a sense of desertion which becomes tangible and oppressive like a vast sweaty palm stretched low across the sky. A weight bears down on them. The air dense and insufferable now the bustle of movement and the throes of active commerce have been blown from the city's vortex, succeeded by this stale and stupefied redundancy. This is not a sight anyone would care an instant for.

He has not been into the city itself since fleeing a week back. How the atmosphere has changed since then. He had left in a deluge of panic and chaos with cars and lorries and buses thronging the streets and backing up along the highways to make their escapes, hooting and jamming each other in. Then the streaming hordes were loping out along the highways on foot or on bicycles, all straddled with the wares of their lives. Children being dragged at heel and babies bundled tight to their mothers' burly backs. Some lugged a clutch of chickens aflutter in makeshift coops; others yanked skittish goats along behind them. Others just left with nothing. The old, the infirm, the sick and dying, too. All souls with half a whim left for life scuttled out like crabs along an oil-slicked beach. He didn't leave with the masses along that shambling noon highway. Too encumbering, too startling. He chose the back road warrens. It turned out much easier that way.

He had woven through the suburbs and then out on the quieter roads. At this point the fighting hadn't broken out fully in the city and the shanties orbiting it, but everyone knew it was coming. He walked and walked and covered a fair distance in a short period of time. He took refuge in a horticultural plantation on the city's outskirts where he kept himself hidden low in the cool green growth, among the lush stalks and rows of budding icebergs, the fragrance ripe and full at his nose. For a while this was heaven. He would have been content to live out his last days in such a place, surrounded by some vague notion of beauty that he hardly understood; untouched, unhampered by man and his war machines.

Then the sounds broke in the still hot air. One moment, late on a cloudless day. The low concussions of mortars and grenades rocking through the ground and the tight chill to the skin in their aftermath each and every time. In the evenings he crept atop a small kopje that was well treed and from there he could look over towards the city. As the sun sank in the sky and the pining evening blueness came to being, he stood there and stared out at the plumes of smoke, the flashes of gunfire, listening to the booms and roars and spatter.

After a few days the noises stopped although great wafts of black smoke still rose over the city, so thick at first they looked like thunder clouds smudging the calm paleness. When it seemed certain the volleying blasts were over, he dislodged himself from the kopje and scrounged around the plantation for food and water, finding little. There was a reservoir he could drink from; what a travesty he couldn't eat roses or sunflowers. He was feeling weak and nuzzled with delirium.

On the fourth day his confidence rekindled and he moved into a well-kempt garden to scrump some plump peaches from a tree. He picked them and was savouring the sharp sweetness on his tongue when an elderly white man came charging at him from the confines of a grand old Cape Dutch house. He was startled because such a stillness had been awash over everything and the plantation seemed long deserted. The man shouted and picked up a handful of stones from the gravel driveway and started pelting him with them, waving his arms and yelling so much his bald head flushed a sweaty crimson. All for a peach or two. In that moment he knew of no way to implore the man to some sympathy and so he ran off into the undergrowth. He roamed around panic-stricken for a while looking for food before coming across that oasis of a vegetable patch on the edge of the shanty town.

They lead him into the city centre. The danger here is inestimable and for a while his trepidation builds again until he can feel his feet grow heavy, wanting to dig into the tar. His whole body recoils into itself. The rope tautens. One of his captors looks back and grimaces at him. He sees a hand tighten round the handle of the machete, its gore-stained blade briefly shimmering as it draws on the sun. There is a grunt and a hard yank down on the rope. It digs into him as the lasso bites. One fear outstrips the other; his legs soften and passively he walks on.

In the city some of the buildings stand shelled, their windows blown out and their roofs caved in from the intense pressure of the fires that have ravaged them. Paint has been singed off large tracts of walls and in some places the structures have begun to collapse, leaving great snaking shafts of bent metal struts bare through the crumbled concrete. Occasionally, a gaping hole through which he can see the remnants of an office appears, as if some keen child has swung open a doll's house. There are charts still pinned to the walls, desks and swivel chairs and pot plants and water purifiers and filing cabinets, all standing there as if in states of shock. Other buildings are untouched, their neat outer facades prim and pristine and their silver windows emblazoned where the bright sunlight of the afternoon smashes into them, dazzling the eyes of onlookers below. But over everything there is a great aura of stagnant alarm as if a vast omnipotent hand has reached out and pressed a pause button in the middle of some urgent action.

The aura of desertion saturates the city entirely. Beyond it there is the sense of something festering in the air, the remnants of some frenzied chaos which broke full into the streets and spilt across the roads and sidewalks and alleyways. On both sides of the street the shop fronts stand battered, their iron girders mangled and their chains hacked. TV sets, hi-fis, DVD players – such easy pickings when the shopkeeper has long fled and the police are busying themselves for the army's assault on the city. Those few days must have felt like paradise. Lugging out their booty and sloping off bleary-eyed or else standing along the pavements guarding it and bartering it off and fighting amongst one another in ways learnt only in the gangland shanties and ghettos. There has been no food on the shelves for many months; DVD players, not food. It is possible to believe that the tatty children were there nonetheless, crawling about the old bakery floors or chain stores and rummaging in storerooms in the back to scoop up the spillage from a long-popped chip packet or a ripped bag of millet, maize, soya.

Then this great vacant space is broken by rapid gunfire blurts from the depths of the rubble. Electric disarray. The fracturing pavement, the blistering tarmac. The trio shout, darting and yanking him. In the flourish of confusion they sidle into an alleyway and duck down behind dustbins spilling with shredded paper. The absurdity and the fragility of it. Agitated exclamations and brief grimaces from one to the other of some unknown fear. No dustbin for him. He tries to press himself against the wall but realizes the stark prominence of himself there. A step into the alleyway and the shadowy marksman will have him sighted. But the gunfire spurt is brief; silence now but for the spreading ring of panic in his ears. The report is a distant hammering quake in his chest. He huddles into the dank slimy stockade and together they all crouch there for some time, looking and listening out at the empty, voided street.

Most likely they're unseen rival factions who have laid siege to this particular quarter of the city. Anything to defend their territory. Or snipers lying hidden behind overturned cars taking pot shots at the legs of pedestrians. For some time anyway he had been walking gingerly, somehow sensing to fear having his kneecaps blown out or his shins blasted. The sound of the gun has been lodged in his ears these last few days: its pop and rip an instant fright to him. How foolish of these men to have ventured into the very sinews of a battlefield.

He had begun to sense what it was like to be shot at, to be shot; there in the blooming plantation when he heard those first far-away booms volley deep towards the shielding sky, then the crackling peal of the automatics in ever responding raps, the monotonous drone purling towards him in faint pulses as if the ground beneath him were giving up murmurs of its deepest self. The back of his throat had a dryness not entirely down to thirst. Some parchment of dull anxiety, the thickening settlement of fear. He would sleep in snatches, curled in the undergrowth, his flesh all the while tingling to the half-expectant stab of wayward bullets. Something falling out of the air. He would feel his eyes flicker in their sockets, knowing the unease of his mind. The nerve endings in his flesh stabbed at him.

When he was chased from the plantation his trepidation grew more marked and at times, when the blasts burst out again and the rifle fire responded, he found he could hardly put one foot in front of the other, so overcome was he with an instant paralysis. He had faltered on, tramping along in his own marcescent way.

It was surprising that he made it to the vegetable patch at all. Surprising, too, that at the point of capture he didn't feel so afraid. Perhaps by then he had sated all his dread and the dull quaking in his throat was just plain hunger and resignation.

After some time they disengage from the bins and regroup in the alley. There is anger and frustration between them. He stands looking on but it doesn't occur to him to take the chance to flee. He isn't thinking like that. Scampering out of the alley and into the sights of the snipers is no option. He doesn't move. Something keeps him nailed to the spot and for the smallest shred of time there in this dark corridor he may have stopped breathing altogether.

One of the militia crawls to the end of the alley, then crawls all the way to the other end and looks out. Crouched like a lizard, he scans the area thoroughly. Not a glimmer to be seen. After a while he returns to give his report. There is much discussion in whispered, agitated tones. Then what sounds like an argument between two of the men, leering at one another with fists clenched. They find themselves trapped and have little way of knowing what to do next. One of them leads the way towards the back end of the alley.

The still, starched air draws them closer to the vacuum of no man's land, a dimension of space where perhaps not a single living entity dares draw a breath. Inch by inch they sidle out, the men scanning the holed-out windows of the adjacent buildings, looking up to the canted rooftops. There isn't a sound that man would know; just the horror of emptiness and silence. He takes a deep breath as the rope yanks him forwards into the open light. The men hurry now, scurrying rats in the undergrowth. He is not as agile. He lumbers behind, dragged by the last of the three men, the rope cutting into his neck, his feet making a noise on the concrete. He thinks he feels a certain heat open up on his back, a radiating space big as a target board so conspicuous that any bored enfeebled sniper would be mad to pass up a pot shot at. But he keeps on moving. There is nothing else to do.

They round the side of the building and emerge onto an adjacent street. They make a dash for another alley and run its dark tunnel, then work their way around the back of a building and then another alley until they have networked well away from the city centre. They do not encounter another human being. The air at last softens and finally they stop and rest against a tall red-bricked wall. They are panting and clearly relieved. But they don't hang around long. On they go, dragging him in their stern by the rope. Out down a deserted street heading west and then down a jacaranda-lined road where the soft scatter of purple flowers is a pleasant distraction, a luscious carpet under his feet. The air is infused with a citrus scent which burrows deep into his nose – even beyond the stench of the gag – and makes him think insatiably of food and those vegetables he was cruelly deprived of.

Eventually they leave the city centre behind and move into the rolling suburbs where high walls, green pavements and lines of tall firs hem their path. A strange sense of calm pervades here. The white people had quietly packed a suitcase, loaded up their cars and driven off to avoid the bother and tedium of the revolt. They are now sitting up in the lush wooded highlands, in stone chalets or log cabins, sipping gin and tonics, snacking on cheese biscuits while looking out over the grey receding tranquillity of a lake. In a while, when the evening chill rises, they will move indoors in front of lilting fires, spitting and crackling through wet logs of pine. They aren't thinking of the civil war, but they are. They are telling one another it's all going to be fine, but they don't believe it.

It was different for him. He wasn't able to pack up and drive off. Caught up in the sudden wave of confusion, things suddenly escalating about him, he walked around for some time not really sure of anything. It was all a fraction removed from him; his mind clouded with an irrepressible despondency, lost in some catalepsy of thought. For a while it was as if things were happening around him in quick, sporadic glitches of unravelling importance which he failed to grasp. Only some days later did he come to the understanding that he ought to sidestep the hubbub and pace his way out of the city before it was too late altogether. Before someone saw him and hewed him down. Before someone in their inhuman desperation (God forbid) ate him. Before a bunch of thugs threw a lasso and captured him.

*

As they lead him past the houses he looks in at the high electric gates and occasionally he can see the large houses hidden away in the shadowy splurge of the gardens. But there is no sign of life. No sign, therefore, of possible rescue. Every now and then a pair of large, jaw-snapping dogs comes charging the gate as they pass, salivating and foaming at the mouth from lack of food and water. They have been left behind in the panic, or maybe on purpose as a deterrent to the looters. There is something redundant about their fierce loyalty. They will be dead in a day or two, hacked down mid bark or leap, their bones licked clean for meat, their hides scraped, salted, baked dry in the sun, stitched into clothes that the limping survivors of the genocide will strap around them.

Past the expansive suburbs and beyond the manicured golf course where the flags on the greens still wave when the wind blows; they walk the roadside and encounter few people. Those they do come across veer to the other side of the road and slink past them cowering. Or they are seen in the distance and are gone in an instant, slipping down the side roads, creeping down into the ditches where they disappear behind a mesh of bush. No cars. No rickety bicycles that are easy targets for three thugs to chase and snatch. They walk for some time. The sun licks the asphalt, spooling back at them in refractory waves. It is midday or just past it. Other bandits may have quartered themselves away from the nakedness of the noontime blink, holing up in shacks and makeshift shanties, but they carry on walking as if on a journey out of the world itself. He is tired but doesn't falter. His captors are tired, too, but they don't show it. The man who leads him tugs on the rope. It makes a tight line between them along which runs a constant menacing pulse. He can feel the vibration at his neck.

They turn off the main road, make a few turns down side roads and continue walking. From behind them a lone figure appears, hobbling along the track and gesturing to them, calling out for them to stop. The men halt and draw their blades and call back. The figure comes limping up, his bare hands raised in the air. He is an old man with bad hips or a bad leg and a silvering mat of hair. He wears the khaki uniform of a domestic servant. His cheeks are fat; he has large pale eyes which are genial and carry no threat. The men relax. They stand and talk for a while. Gestures are exchanged. The old man points up the road and beckons them to follow. After a while they turn around and walk with this old man who keeps chatting amiably while looking him up and down out the corner of his eyes. All through the short journey this man casts a constant possessive glare over him and he doesn't like it.

They arrive at the gate of a large property, slab-walled with a concreted seal of broken glass. The gate is high and barred. The old man wheels it back and ushers them in. The yard is vast and vacant. No dogs yap at their arrival but he has a feeling still that this is marked territory. The brick drive winds elegantly to a double-door garage and, beside it, a house that looks cool and newly whitewashed. It has a black roof and wide French doors and windows with rosebushes sprawling beneath them. The lawn has begun to overgrow. The dead flowers in the beds lining the driveway droop from their stalks or have fallen and lie crushed on the tarmac. The pool has begun to turn green; its rim heaves with a mulch of leaves. Otherwise it's an ordinary suburban home. They make their way up to the house and stop by a long glitter-stone porch with white-enamelled railings.

They tie him by the rope to a pole and he stands there looking on. He has no comprehension of what they have come here to do. He tries to inch back on the rope but the knot only tightens. He can only stand and watch what unfolds, bear witness to acts from which he is excluded. His dimming mind is growing ever more passive as the day wears on. It rests somewhere on the edge of indolence, nestled blissfully in a vegetable patch or a peach tree. Only skittering motions of violence or danger will dislodge it. The old man fishes a key from his pocket and shows it off to the men. They crowd round as he unlocks the door and burst into the lounge. The old cookboy is knocked to the ground.

They comb the house, the old man piteously wobbling after them in turns, calling after the beasts he has unleashed on his master's home, pleading with them to restrain themselves. He can see them from the porch, streaming up and down the passage, in and out of the lounge. They push the old man out of the way and dismiss his pleas. There are tall framed photographs of smiling white faces sitting on the TV cabinet until they're brushed off with an urgent swipe and shatter crisply on the ceramic floor. Books are pulled from shelves, ornaments go flying, furniture is shunted about. The old man backs away to the porch door and stands there looking on.

The house is trashed from the inside out. In the orgy of looting a spate of fighting breaks out: two of them have laid claim to a DVD player and tug it back and forth between their clenched fists, their voices snarling at one another. One strains forward and slams the other into a wall. There is a thud; an oil landscape tilts on its hook and slides to one side. It takes the third man to calm them down and stop an all-out brawl. In the relative sanity that follows, they gather their booty and bring it out onto the porch. A small flatscreen TV, a laptop, a digital camera, the DVD player.

The old man stands, his face and eyes glazed over. The hard lead weight of his betrayal. He looks at his trade, tied there frail and meek to the pole. He looks over the stack of merchandise. There is a grim silence as the men make one last sweep of the house. Then they lug their pickings off down the drive, an easy swagger in their step. The old man watches them disappear up the road and then locks up the house, slips the key into his pocket and unties him from the pole.

He cares little for what has just happened. He has no great opinion about it beyond the raw facts, its bland happening. The old man limps away with him round the back of the house, past the garage and down a little narrow path towards the kias which are nestled behind a spilling compost heap and a tin garden shack with tendrils of moss growing up the base. The old man hardly looks at him now but ties him to the branch of a lemon tree and then sits down on a shoddy wooden stool outside the door to the kia room. Now that there are only two of them he begins to moan and struggle in the grip of the rope and the foul gag, but the old man doesn't seem in the mood for granting a little sympathetic respite. Just a little hunched man sitting there brooding and staring ahead as if the world and its sins has suddenly blinded him, as if he stares on nothing but darkness now, tanned with the dimmest infusion of the sun.

After a while, the old man gets up and limps to the side of his kia and bends to scoop up a sadza-caked pot. He carries it over to a tap spurting like a flower from a patch of green button weeds and begins to scour it with a wire brush. The suds of sadza clot and loosen, pooling into scum which he tips down a drain, speckling it white with dripping slime. He leans the pot against the wall and peels some shoots of rape which he heaps into a bundle. He lumbers off his stool again and shuffles inside the dark cube of his room.

He is quiet for a time. The gloom furls out, an insidious gas, vaporized instantly by the chinks of sun piercing the lemon tree and the hedge against the wall. Suddenly there is a great sharp whack of a blade against a chopping board. It slices through him. He shudders from the inside out. A grey dove takes flight from the tree, scatters up against the blueness of the day and vanishes. Another pelt of the blade and this time he hears the steel rend. He strains in the harness and pulls hard against the tree. The rope jams and grips his neck and his shoulder blades. A sharp pain cuts into him. The thin bow of the trunk lilts but will not give. He starts shaking his head but the ropes are unforgiving. Now the old man is at his side shouting at him and grappling at the ropes to steady him. From the corner of his eye he catches sight of the meat cleaver raised and ready to strike and he cowers down against the tree.

The threat is enough to still him. He stands uneasily, breathing heavily and panting through the gag. His breath is steamy and hot, wheeling about his mouth. His feet feel impermanent. The old man moves back inside his room. Soon there is the dull clanking sound of metal bashing against brick. When the man walks out again he's carrying a stainless steel dish which he places on the ground. Inside lies the rump and hindquarter of some small beast glistening darkly in a stow of blood. It looks muscled and lean with a pointed foot that's been half hacked away. Blood pools from the flesh in an accumulated silence. The old man squats by the tap and fills the pot to half. He presses in the rape and sets it aside. Then he moves over to a small paraffin cooker stacked atop some charred bricks and fiddles with the valves before taking a

box of matches from his pocket and lighting the plate. It flares in
a low blue flame. The rape boils away and when it's reduced some
he adds more water before laying in the hindquarter. It bubbles
and spatters. The stench of the dark meat gluts the air.

The old man tears the withered rape leaves and picks at the
grey hindquarter. He rolls them into balls and chews them stren-
uously. He sits consuming his meal while his new acquisition
stands tied to a tree looking on it all. When he is finished lapping
up the juices with the last of the leaves he rinses out the pot and
stands it to drain. Then he takes the bone over to a garbage pile
heaped up beside a vegetable bed where limp green stacks of rape
sprout. He tosses the bone and a pocket of flies bursts out and scatters momentarily before diving back to a small pelt of beige and
white fur that hangs over the branch of an avocado tree. The old
man limps back again and looks him up and down and then goes
off to his room. There descends a long and rigid quiet.

He looks at the tap and the circle of damp beneath it and can feel
the thirst harden in his mouth. He has been standing for some
time. His legs are tired. His mouth is numb. There is a dull ache
nudging the corners of his eyes. He manages to shift his stance
and turn himself around. He eyes up the garden, the back of the
house, the driveway running crisply to the gate and can sense the
open road. He knows he should try and make good an escape
before the old man wakes up and comes out of his room and starts
looking him up and down with vague insinuations. He looks
closely at the knots that bind him, he bends forward and tries to
gnaw at one with his teeth, but the gag is too tight: he can barely
open his mouth. Shifting, he strains again, trying to bend the
branch to a point where it will snap. But it won't. He eases up and

stands there. Then, ahead of him he sees two youths standing and watching. They have jumped over the wall from the neighbouring house.

They are in their early teens but look hardened, carrying sacks on their backs with machetes belted to them. They whisper to one another and he can't hear them. These boys look surprised to see him tied there; disbelieving, in a contented sort of way, as if they'd stumbled on a store of wealth. As they come towards him his body tenses up. He tries to cringe into himself but he is unable to. Then there is a sound to the right of them and the old man is standing at his doorway. He starts to shout and gesticulate, lumbering forward, but one of the boys has already lunged out and struck him across the throat. The blood thickens quickly. The old man gargles and splutters, staggering back against the wall where he slides to the ground leaving a swathe of blood smeared bright against the brickwork.

In the racking stillness of those next moments, neither boy seems to know what to do. They look at the old man's body slumped against the wall, the blood still spilling in jets from the gash at his throat. It seems that only when the jets slow to a trickle do they register their act and are quick to extricate themselves from it. They untie him from the tree and pull him along with them. In shock, his legs stumble on mechanically and he doesn't put up any protest.

They had come to ransack houses but they are leaving with a bigger prize – a living being. They move down the driveway and pull the gate back on its coaster, relieved to find it's not locked. It's as if they want to get out quick so the next marauders who scale the wall won't find what they've found. It is bewildering to him why they would want to take him hostage. He has no concept of his value in this order of things. Still, the three of them move briskly down the deserted road and quickly make a turn left and then they turn left again onto what seems like a wider, more public road. But it is deserted. The hot eeriness of a fairground park after hours, thronging with the buzz of its daytime crowds.

They hurry along, almost at a trot, pulling him behind them. It's as if something may swerve round the corner at any second and store them in their sights: some murderous, militant gang. They quickly veer off towards a small shopping centre. It too is deserted save for the odd car caught unawares in the lot, windscreens webbed and sagging from a pelting. The ransacked bottle store; the butchery; the fruit and veggie mart; the pharmacy. Red plastic shopping baskets lie cracked, scattered at the entrances. Giant dominoes of white enamelled shelves lie toppled into each other. The mannequins in the small boutique lie naked and grotesquely abused on beds of glass. He is pulled round the back of the complex where a stinking stretch of potholed tar covers the ground between the delivery zones of the shops and a white-washed wall now grey with grime and graffiti. The puckered tar has blades of beige grass sticking up through it like sails on paper boats and litter spills from large drums and lies decaying in the stagnant sun.

An agitation of flies and then the slimy belly of a rat slides through the scatter and he hardly notices the odd pair standing there in the lot. They seem somehow the limp and tatty product of its squalor. A stocky man of middling height with a stern expressionless face comes striding forward, opens a toothless mouth and a raw sound spews out, some alien lingo. He is strangely drawn to the workings of the man's mouth, opening and closing on a darkness, certain night hours never yet wit-nessed. For a moment he is scared to his skin. And when the man ceases talking a sudden stillness sweeps down. Motions and actions he wasn't aware of stop and fall silent and he feels a malign and concentrated attention push towards him. For an awkward time no one says anything. Not the boys, his captors. Not the strange cast staggered about in this weird and random tableau.

He looks about and surveys the people around him. There are four altogether now: this man, the two boys, and a woman. She is pregnant. The last time he saw a woman was one stone dead in the bushes. She is crouched on the ground, weary eyed. She ignores him. He stares at them all for a heavy moment which may be quite a passing of time or almost none at all.

He senses the man is very pleased with the boys' find, their catch. The boys are smiling, basking in their triumph. He stands there in that dusty quarter with the rope dangling from his neck to the tar. He is a specimen they talk about, scrutinize. They are studying his bones, his physique, his condition. Together they are making an appraisal of him, saying what an asset he will be when the time comes for them to need an asset. Yet despite the humiliation, the conveyed indignity of it, the drive to turn and run from the shopping centre and back down the roads through the suburbs somehow seems devoid in him. It's curled tightly into some wrought place. Perhaps he simply lacks the energy to do so. He stands asunder from the group and watches them with his tired eyes. The rope dappling on the ground. His unshackled being. The gag still packed in his mouth and sitting acridly on his tongue and in the mayhem it seems he has almost relinquished its existence.

The man mutters to one of the youths who walks towards him and picks up the end of the rope and walks him ten paces before fixing it to an iron pole cemented into the concrete ground. The pole forms the corner of a large storage bin and the rotting smells instantly stain the air. Even the boy recoils in disgust and walks away quickly. If only the gag was removed he could at least breathe through his mouth. He should feel sick but he doesn't. He stands there for some time tied to the pole and the discomfort of it and the tiredness in his legs starts to make him moan a little. The muffled sound he invokes is pathetic. No one is roused an instant.

He watches the woman crawl about gathering waste in the lot. She scoops it up in the bow of her baggy dress and hobbles over to a heap of ash and scalded bricks where she stacks it into a tripod, ready to be lit. The man brings out a box of matches from an inner pocket of his trousers. He extracts a single match and strikes down. The match flares and wanes and flares. Some relief is evident. The fuel is lit. The woman squats next to it and begins to roast four maize cobs she has skewered with the spokes of a plundered shopping trolley. He looks on in amazement. Such wealth: a store of cobs casually spiked and stacked atop the flames; the pale yellow gleam of their kernels gently browning, blistering. The smell of charred sweetness.

Still, the smoky whiff of maize may drift too far in the cauterized air and alert some prowling famished gang to their whereabouts. Here any conception is possible. All is stoked by desperation of the lowest order. Some ravaging troop may come bursting over the wall or pounce on them from the tops of the shop buildings. The gangs of rival militias may come across them and their four little cobs and blast them all away. Or the approaching wave of the military – surely at last regrouped and mobilized – may storm the area, round them up and have them declared guilty of treason. They'd be shot in the head at dawn or struck in the gut with a panga if their bullets had by then run out. It would be no small wonderment.

For a while he studies this group with a cautious eye. The man has a sprouting of grey in his beard and his hair. He is fairly well built but thin with a firm, gaunt face and eyes that hint to some steeliness in his character, some depth of soul not for the turning. He wears faded tweed trousers, a grubby white shirt, threadbare at the collar, and a pair of dusty leather shoes. He sizes this man up, scrutinizes him: it is his turn now. It's possible the two adolescents will prove to be the most combative. They seem to be of similar age, twins possibly, and they sit about bare-chested, their charcoal skin drawn tight across their firm bodies, their thighs bulging, their biceps prominent, their calves sculpted and sanded and pumiced from some great hulk of ebony.

The man chats to the boys as if telling stories round a bonfire while the woman continues to turn the browning cobs over the smoky flame. They seem at ease. They seem to believe in their own sense of infallibility, here in the back alleyway of the shops, nestled cosily. The woman presents them with their blackened cobs and then withdraws into the shade of some awning strung up from the back of one of the shops and sits looking out over the cracking asphalt. He sees them biting into the cobs and a first touch of despondency breaks within him. He remains standing for a while longer and when it seems acceptable to do so he sinks to the ground, the rope just loose enough to allow him the flexibility to lower his head and catch a moment's rest.

They sit round all afternoon stoking and feeding the waning fire. Sometimes talking, mostly not. Sometimes listening as a rare truck roars close by, sounding as if it has driven into the parking lot. They wait for the military choppers that blade overhead. They are listening, too, for the blare that comes from the trucks that had of late rolled across the streets and suburbs, loudspeakers wired to their cab tops, a continuous disembodied drone wavering out at the few people who remained, like the grave voice of an embittered god. The trucks had inched street by street, the strange electric voice echoing all about them. Some of the citizens may have thought Armageddon itself was at hand. Some had drifted about dazed and aimless and catatonic, defying the decree to leave the city and return to their tribal lands. They wanted the city flushed. Then some who had dallied were shot on sight and kicked into ditches. Everyone else went into hiding.

The day has been hot and the long walk from the shanties has taken its toll. His shoulders are tight and his limbs ache. His body hankers for a patch of rest but as the sun finally dips down and a dim amber glow spools over the cooling asphalt, they all rouse themselves at the command of the man. The youths have been snoozing on flattened cardboard boxes, the woman at rest under the spread of the tatty awning. One of the youths comes over and unties him from the pole. Not a word is uttered; the boy hardly even looks at him. The men gather themselves. The woman remains sitting. From a stack of sacks and plastic bags one of the boys extracts a broomstick broken in half with a bob of hessian bundled round the top. The boy lowers this handmade torch to the fire and in an instant it flares in a quick wave of blue, then settles down to a weak pulsing flame. The smell of methylated spirits briefly sours the air.

They set off at sunset from the back of the shopping centre. The man, the two boys and he. One boy carries the torch, the other swings an empty twenty-litre plastic water container. The man carries a bundle under his arm, wrapped in a white shopping bag with a red logo on it but he soon slips it under the inner sleeve of a thin navy tracksuit top which he puts on and zips up. The three of them move out, pulling him in their wake, plodding along the quiet roads of the suburbs once again. The branches of trees intertwine overhead tunnelling them in and dousing them in a syrupy light which seems all too confining. It's growing dark

31

quickly and apart from the darting whine of a mosquito, nobody else is about. Even the abandoned dogs have given up their gate patrol.

Over everything there's soon a great spill of darkness and no glimmer of a moon. Not one of the houses seems occupied and when night falls and the crickets finally sing from the lawns, there are no dotted gate lights. No slow flickering street lamps overhead casting waves of dimness up through the netted branches and down on the grimy road. Not even the lowing of a generator breaking the dead stillness of the air. It is just them: four dimly illuminated figures plunging into the darkness. The torchlight is a comfort. He feels a sense of relief that because of the glow he can see what surrounds him. At least things have vague form and the group are not these bodiless beings haranguing him in the dark and pulling him along in the depths of some stuffy dream.

They turn down a road. The trees on the pavements have thinned out and an immediate sense of exposure floods over him. The sky opens up on a covering of dull, distant stars. The lack of light across the city renders the night naked and raw. The sky used to look different – cool and calm and chaste – not this random screen of chaos which now seems to exude some force of misalignment, some pretension. Of course the truth is that the sky is the sky and really it's the blotted fuzziness of his mind that drops it so sharply from focus.

At a T-junction they make a left and then soon afterwards a right into what ends in a close, the road circling a small island of spiky indistinct grass. Three large properties arch around it. They make their way to the one in the middle and stop outside a tall wall stitched along the top with a coiled electric fence and a squat nest of cacti shrubs planted along the bottom. Even in the dark he can see the tips of the thorns glimmering like nails and trace the erectness of the rubbery shoots towards a blurred mass of black. The others stand awhile conferring with one another. The man approaches the tin-boarded electric gate and taps three times. Then he stands back and waits. Whistles quietly. Nothing happens. He knocks. Finally a soft coarse voice calls out from the night and a faint, fluid conversation starts up. He can't understand a word and tension nudges its way into his stomach.

Eventually the gate rolls back a short way on its coaster. The man enters and then the gate rolls closed again and they are left waiting outside those teethed walls. A space of time passes. That dark disjunction of being. Something cold across his soul. At last the gate slides ajar and a whisper brings them in. The property at once gives off the rich scent of wet soil — he is alarmed at the comfort of this. The humid smell fills his lungs and draws him along the driveway, no one need prod him or yank him now.

The moisture is such a pleasant change to the dry dustiness he has been accustomed to that gets up his nose and sits there along with the nebulizing muzzle across his face. The whole garden seems to drip coolness from every branch, from every shrub, fern, plant. Immediately he senses a flow of water nearby. His mouth prickles with anticipation and he is drawn to the sight of a man in tatty overalls and gumboots standing by a flowerbed, holding a hosepipe, drenching the plants and the soil. There is no muffled roar of a generator; there is only an inexplicable silence that incites his bafflement.

Oblivious to constraints he trudges his way over and stands beside the hose, silent and breathless. No one says anything. The man withdraws the plastic bag from under his tracksuit. He opens it and brings out a bag of crushed dried fish. Someone comes up

33

behind them along the driveway. A short man in a grey overcoat. He takes the bag of fish and holds it, running his fingers over the clear plastic, stroking the flaky fillets. Finally he nods to the man holding the hose, slipping the fish underneath his coat and disappearing up the driveway. The man and the boys come forward and drink their fill and then they dip the nozzle of the pipe into the container and they all stand about listening to it drum against the plastic. It curls full to the brim. They screw the cap onto it tightly and one of the boys walks off with it, lopsided now, down the driveway and into the bleary darkness.

All the while he stands there looking on patiently and desperately. It is impossible they will forget him. He is aware of an exchange of bemused glances and then the other boy is beside him, fiddling with the gag. Its release is such relief his vision fuzzes slightly and he feels light on his feet. When he regains focus the man with the hosepipe is looking at him. A moment later he steps forward and brings the nozzle to his mouth like some apostolic baptizer of the night. The spray juts out firm and steady and gushes round his mouth strong as an avalanche.

He drinks and drinks until the hose is pulled away from him. He watches it continue to drench the dark colourless plants. He stands there and gapes bewildered about him and allows the damp night air to be drawn towards his sated tongue and wet face, to sink its soft balminess into his tired brow. Indulged in this luxuriance, his guard lowered, he feels adrift from the actions of his captors. They have disappeared down the driveway and left him. He hears muted voices punctuating the steady spray throbbing from the hosepipe but nonetheless he feels alone and distantly, blissfully frightened. He stands regarding the man watering the flowerbed.

They walk back down the driveway. They pick up the rope and reattach the gag. The gate rolls open and lets them slip out and rolls closed again. There a couple are waiting outside with an array of empty juice bottles, whistling softly for some attention. Briefly their eyes all meet in the bluish halo of the hessian lamp, invisible lasers scanning one another with the deepest scrutiny. Not a sound is uttered between them. They move away from the property and tread along the road. The boy lugging the water container falls some way behind and the man lingers with him. The risk of being seen in the glow is too terrifying to contemplate, so the other boy leads him on and carries the torch as a decoy. He looks like a medieval monk on a lone crusade, stooping across the outlays of some heathen land.

They take a few turns and walk for some while before stopping outside a property with a high brick wall and a line of shadowy palm trees along its pavement. It has an ornate entrance with concrete statues of miniature sphinxes guarding the gates. The boy with the water cowers behind the palms. The man whistles and taps on the high wooden gate. Someone pulls back one half of the unwieldy gate and they step inside. The man moves off at once, sidling along the darkness of hedge. One boy follows after him and then the other boy comes sidewinding into the entrance, rolling the drum of water. The gate closes. All is quiet.

He moves along the driveway to seek his captors out, following the distant hum of voices. There is no inclination to flee: the streets beyond the gate are serpentine, inked with malice. So he moves forward. There is a garage draped in creepers and behind it a shed made from planks, with a strong stench of creosote. He spots them deep in negotiations. His captor and another man.

They gibber animatedly. At times voices are raised and exclamations uttered before they remember themselves and the volume of their speech lowers to an expressive whisper. Then the two men move off behind the house and follow a small brick-lined path towards the rear domestic quarters. He stands looking about. The house is an imposing double-storey; the darkened sheen of the windows gives it an eerie presence. It is possible people may actually be behind those windows even now looking down into the garden at his shape in the dark and wondering strange things.

There is squeaking along the path. The men return pushing a weird and cumbersome contraption. It lollops ungraciously along the uneven brickwork and then comes into full view. Two small wheels with fat tyres are attached to a chassis and the chassis is welded to a frame of sorts on which is fixed a wrought-iron cab or compartment. It looks exactly the same as the ice boxes the ice-cream men used to push or the portable bread bins the bread vendors used to station at street corners. Just bigger. They draw it to a halt near him. He looks down at the compartment which is decked out with warped wooden plywood planks. Leading from the chassis are two poles in an A-frame and where the two poles meet, a toe hitch. Its creator stands over it protectively, still prodding bits into place, holding a complex network of ropes and harnesses. He has some inclination what is about to happen next.

The two youths come behind him, grip him by the shoulders and turn him around. He tries to struggle but they shout, *Hey hey hey,* and he feels the flat of a hand slap him across the back of his neck. The pain inches into him so he stands still. The gag is re-attached and tied tight behind his head. A weight comes down on his back, straddling his neck. Within a few seconds the whole thing is fixed, the ropes bound round his chest and shoulders. An unknowing feeling of despair comes over him. There is a thud behind him and he sees they've dumped the water container into the compartment. Someone pushes him in the back; he feels a sharp punch to his ribs. *Shoo, shoo,* the boy says, gesturing him to walk. Wide eyed and startled he moves forward and feels the weight of the contraption strain against him. He tries again. The boy slaps him in the ribs again and he lunges forward grimacing as the whole ungainly mechanism moves along the driveway after him bobbing like some gangly old chimp in a circus show.

Even the short trip back to the shopping centre is taxing. The wheels are fat but slight in circumference and the sheer inconstancy of them fails to grip the tar. They have not been mounted properly; they wobble and shake. The chassis has no suspension to speak of so the weight of the compartment and the axle pounds into him whenever the tyres slip into the smallest divot, sending a battery of shocks through his spine. Hitting a pothole will be calamitous. He walks with his eyes trained to the tarmac, scanning in the dim glow.

Back across those goffered tracks they tramp in the dark, through the cavernous tunnels of trees, beneath the icy distant spew of stars, the absent moon. Nothing moves out there except their motley troop. Those three stooges and he and the cart behind him whining and slurping over the black pool of roads. Some way before they reach the shopping centre the hessian torch hisses and flickers and burns out and that weak blue flame is extinguished forever. So they inch onwards unsighted in the shudder of those night-time sounds.

At the hideout the woman squats again over a small flame roasting cobs behind a screen of cardboard boxes. The boys extract the water container, undo the cart and wheel it parallel to a wire cage which towers with crates of empty bottles. They tie him again to the pole and soon he sinks to the ground, exhausted. His breathing is laboured. The men chew on their cobs and if they speak at all he cannot hear them. Blood is drumming in his ears, everything now a fraction removed from him, a fraction distorted, dulled, deadened. The woman retreats into the dark. He cannot see her now; only the men chewing away.

He lies there at his uncomfortable station, edging his weary spine against the grooves of the cage for some support. He looks about with listless eyes, the stencilled shapes of the figures blurring now and then, the fire's pull weakening. On occasion he hears odd sounds close by: the scurry of vermin, probing mosquitoes. Once an empty bottle topples on concrete somewhere, shattering the taut stillness. One of the boys is sent to investigate and comes stumbling by, swooned in lethargy, his eyes half succumbed to sleep, a line of drool crusted down his chin. He tries to extend his hearing beyond the lot and out into the wide furling night but there he can only determine a warm thrumming stagnancy. He tries to spool his senses into the asphalt to discern the distant shudder of tanks rolling quietly into town or the collected thud of soldiers' marching boots stamping crisp across the roads but he can detect nothing.

Some indistinguishable time later a low hiss bores its way into his ears and he looks across the lot at a figure hunched in the dark. His eyes accustom themselves to the sight of the man cradling a small radio, thumbing at the knob. The boys sit round like elders at a tribal council. A slew of words here and there between the hissing and bleeping. All gibberish to him. They thumb on. Then finally a string of speech. The set is raised to the man's ears. He lowers his head and closes his eyes and they all sit listening. They exclaim intermittently. The occasional shake of the head. Some stuttered disbelief. Then the words dissolve into strains of traditional music, tinny and jerky, and they click the radio off and fold up its aerial, slipping it back into a sack.

The group sit mumbling. The odd traditional tune hummed in that hooded cloister. Phrases of bush lore. Perhaps some calling on the ancestors. One by one they drop off, lying curled against one another on the cardboard tarps and raggedy bags. He puts his head down and allows the world to dislodge around him. He dozes. He wakes. He dozes.

At some point he hears whispered discussion and raises his consciousness from the dank concrete terrain to see the man standing and instructing the boys, gesturing and pointing. The boys clutch something pliable and the man bends towards the clutter round the fire and brings out the length of a machete. He sees its cold blade glint in the dimness and something in him stiffens. One of the boys takes the machete and together with his cohort slips off into the dark while the man looks on after them. He stands there for a long time watching, even after their disseminated bodies have waned in the shroud of night and there is nothing except the presence of their actions reeling against the fears of his mind. It is some time before the man breaks his stare and steals back to his cardboard mattress.

He may sleep only lightly after this. He may not sleep at all. Probing shivers of anxiety and fear spill across his flesh. Hours later he hears a distinct whistle and thinks it must be birdsong heralding the dawn. Nothing so innocent. The man leaps up from his curled state and rushes from view. A pause in which every imagined horror riles him. He huddles against the cage. As he cowers down, the rope tautens. Then they all return – the man, the two boys – tramping in a line like silhouettes shorn of the soul.

They lug bloated sacks across their shoulders like gross deformities. They swing them from their backs and the staccato clank of tin against the iron casement of a rubbish dumpster placates his thoughts, wanes his fear. He loses interest in their operation and from then on he is only conscious of odd movements about him and at times a strange flitting presence which seems to be standing over him and observing him. Perhaps it's one of the group checking to see he has not fled in the night. That he has not bitten through the gag and wrestled free from the ropes and slunk his furtive shadow into the abyss. Or maybe all this is some machination of the mind, some conjured fear made tangible on the sterile night air.

Dawn comes in the end. Then the blaze of the full morning sun cruel and bright on the grey turf. No birdsong in the suburbs that he can hear. No jostling sounds from the streets: the sweep of morning traffic or the brisk rush to work. He fixes his eyes on the ropes that dangle round him and drape on the asphalt where he lies – the stolid assurance of his reality. Already the men are up, sitting on the boxes with the loose sacks swathed across their shoulders, staring out over the vacant lot as if this moment dawned over each of them with the full weight of some unsolvable quandary. There is no sign of the woman.

They dig about in the guts of a large waste dumpster and unearth a heap of tatty bags and plastic packets. The bags are stuffed with rags and clothing, spilling with food the boys have plundered in some vicious raid he doesn't care to think on. Tins of relish, baked beans. Bags of dried fish, rice and grain. One or two luxuries: a bottle of cooking oil, a tin of paraffin, a black cooking pot. He stands there as the boys wheel out the cart and station it behind him. They hardly glance at him. The harness is attached; the ropes bundled tighter round his chest.

The woman appears from round the back of the dumpster and hobbles across the asphalt, gripping the ball of her swollen stomach as she idles towards him. Her breathing is laboured. Screeds of discomfort flush across her face. She stands by the cart, her hands pressed into her back. The man packs the cab with cardboard and rags and then slowly helps her ease her way in. The cart sags under the immediate strain of it; the wheels buckle some. She sits with her legs raised over the edges of the compartment, the weight of her pregnant stomach rising from her like a bulb.

The rest of the group gather themselves, the provisions slung over their shoulders or somehow tied to their backs. The heavier sacks are stashed beside the woman in the cart and the water container is wedged between her legs. The wheels strain and fret, the chassis bulging beneath it all. One of the boys slaps him on the back with the flat of a machete. Pain darts towards his spine and splinters outwards across his body. He lurches forwards, digging into the ground with his legs. The strain of it. The cart rocks gently back and forth. He lunges again, feeling the ropes cut across his chest, neck, shoulders.

All he knows is fear for the flight of the machete through the quickening air at his straining neck. There is nothing comprehensible about what lies ahead. The distance is unknown to him, the scale of the torment yet to be borne. The woman grits her teeth and grips the cart, legs flung immodestly outwards. How long, in her condition, can she tolerate the thumps of the ride before her womb yields and her waters soak the planks beneath her? He has no assurance that within a mile, maybe half that, she'll be screaming in pain or that the birth, messy and fatal at the side of the road, will be the only way they realize their stupidity and draw a halt to the journey before it has begun.

Off they go, shuffling from the stinking shopping centre and onto the side roads. No matter how shaky the ride becomes and how many divots the cart falters through, the woman hangs on with a steely resolve, holding her stomach and pulling wearisome faces, leaking the odd anguished groan. Her muscles must be as tough as rubber, her tendons as strong as wire.

Once momentum is established, the cart is not unbearably heavy to pull. The problem arises whenever they slow and the cart's centre of balance is disturbed. Then, the whole contraption comes careening into his legs, or the front tilts abruptly, digging into the ground and causing the woman to shout out in anguished discomfort. It is not his fault. The men don't always see it this way and on occasion they grow petulant with him. He is hit hard across the side of his head and for a moment the grey road floats and froths as if a hot spring pooled beneath his feet. His eyes water over and he has no words to protest his alarm. He staggers on.

The city is flat for the most part, straddled atop an expansive plateau. It only undulates occasionally, rising and dipping over moderate inclines or hillocks. When they face such a rise it's a labour and a half. He feels the cart begin to strain and its weight moil and then the harness bites into his shoulders and a ten-tonne granite boulder may well be what he drags in his wake. The world is at his shoulders. But such slogging is nothing compared to the perils of any descent. He is lucky not to suffer serious injury to his legs. The boys walk alongside and when they see the cart wheel out of control they step in and pull backwards on it to ease the descent. Sometimes it's a close call. Sometimes they put stones under the wheels to act as a brake. Sometimes after such ordeals they bring the whole trap to a halt and allow him a moment to compose himself.

They go on like this for some time and the woman hunkers down and holds steady. She doesn't cry except for the occasional burst of whimpering. The rest of the group plod on grimly. On the flat stretches the boys run some way ahead of their path and, gripping the machetes in their fists, they survey the terrain for bandits lying in wait to ambush them. The man keeps a steely eye about him. If the boys lower the machete parallel to their legs then passage is safe. If it is raised to shoulder height it's a signal to halt whilst the boys make further investigations, often hunched down and crawling to the nearest cul-de-sac or gate post or hedge and then inching forward like spies or snakes in the undergrowth. When they come to a T-junction, they halt automatically some thirty or so yards before whilst the boys make a full reconnaissance of the coming bend or turn. The whole while the man glances behind them to make sure no one is sneaking up on them from the rear.

Sometimes the man drops the rope and walks alongside the cart and mutters words to the tender-bellied woman. For the most part they take inconspicuous back roads, sometimes winding round in a near circle to avoid the obvious dangers present on the main highways. Sometimes they encounter slim streams of pedestrians but long before their paths cross, the boys have confronted them and made them account for their intentions. Sometimes they are wary of approaching groups and quickly make a turn or a detour. Mostly the roads are deserted and so they inch onwards.

Then they are set on by a trio of militia. Tall, striding men dressed in long grey khaki coats leer towards them on their left flank. They appear from nowhere and the fright of it is instant, a shock through his whole self. He stops dead in his tracks. The woman's panting screams blunt the air and he sees the boys running back to them, brandishing their blades and yelling, but the attackers already have theirs poised and gripped double-fisted, trained within a few feet of them.

There is a stern holler and the boys freeze mid-motion, standing posed in attitudes half-ready to lunge or flee. They look to the man and the attackers alternately confused and frightened. The man steps forward with his bare hands held out and tries to talk, but the machete tenses in the bandit's fist and he stills himself. The trio circle in on them, glancing over their strange set-up with the blankest interest. His breath punctures into quickening gasps but outwardly he remains passive and immobile as a snake in the grasses. The negotiations are tense and frayed and it is only when the man points to the woman and she presses the outline of her belly do the bandits utter the briefest of exclamations. One of them strokes his chin and nods indifferently. Waves of relief spread over them all. The boys lower their machetes; the bandits do, too. There is some savouring calm. They poke around the knapsacks and prod at their pockets, helping themselves to two bags of dried fish and a jar of peanut butter before waving them on again. The group totters forward and no one looks back for an instant.

Their progress is even slower after this. The man mutters to the boys and scolds them. They look ashamed at the encounter and walk on sulkily. After a few hours they come to the edge of the city. The sun is blazing down now. They don't come across any other trouble. Only two cars tear by the whole morning, neither one military or police.

When they get to the outer suburbs the houses start looking more battered. Gates have been bashed down and the slabs of concrete walling smashed in with what looks to have been the rams of armoured vehicles, exposing the houses which show their injuries like victims lying destitute after some natural scourge. There's a barrage of damage: broken windows, tiles torn from the roofs, grids bent in, burglar bars contorted. No animals here. No scampering dogs. No fowl aflutter in the gardens.

Once or twice one of the boys is sent into the more affluent-looking properties to scavenge for provisions, but he comes back empty handed. There is nothing left that could be carried by the hands of man; these places were scoured clean days ago. But a few houses later a pillow and some bedding are unearthed. The boy comes running out with glinting eyes, a widening grin. The man glances over the prize. The pillow is smeared with a crust of red which flakes off crisply when the man scratches at it with his fingernails. The dark mottled blanket hides its defilements. He folds the pillow onto its stain and tenderly packs it behind the woman's back. The blanket he folds and eases under her buttocks. On they tramp.

On the edge of the city some houses are mere shells, black and buckled, scarred wide across their red seared brick, roofing collapsed into great sooty cavities where the tiles lie shattered like scorified sprees of larva. Over everything this mordant splurge. When at last these properties thin out they cross a narrow plain – a dumping ground interspersed with clumps of dry grass – and beyond that the levelled expanse of a shanty towns comes once again into view. These towns are different to the ones he traipsed through yesterday. Still there is little difference to the sight here. The smoke billows from the scorched metal and thatch and riddled plastic sheeting. The smells sour the air. They halt for a good minute and look over the carnage, sullen and bewildered. They mutter and exclaim. The extent of it all, the scale. They seem glum-struck by it. The woman begins to sob, gently at first, and then breaking into loud, breathless wailing. Slowly, amidst this anguished requiem, they move on.

They do not stop again to dwell on the destruction but keep a stoical poise throughout their trail across the wasteland. Occasionally here and there they come across the grim sight of a limb sticking up through the debris, an arm or a leg, sometimes a stretch of skin that may be a belly or a back, always burnt crisp, the blood dried black. Always the man stiffens first and tries to veer them off onto another route or path but sights of the genocide are inevitable. The image of flesh gorged by flames, hardly inseparable from the rags and sheeting and scorched tin, yet always an instant pull on the eyes as if the brain is being drawn there to register the bloody and evil ways of man. The stench is unbearable; the air stained with tarry flesh smells blazed in the open, the heady congealment of blood and fluids, the harried soul spilling into the stagnancy, newly fled from a slashing or a beheading or a burning. Hanging there intermingled with the smoke, dumb and befuddled.

There in that great vacancy is the bareness of being. Plodding through those once-peopled killing fields they inch along the tendrils of some encompassing dread. Nothing they have ever known matches the senselessness of that sight. The sheer scar of vitriol. There seems no other way to go now they are in the middle of it. They have not chosen a route around the cooling inferno to avert bearing witness to this display of misery and desolation: they are amidst it, fording it. The boys keep having to clear a way for the cart, moving tin and brick and a clattering of junk spewed into the dirt tracts. In some areas the trail is smoothed by natural attrition. In others its tedium is overbearingly torturous. For some stretches then he may close his eyes to the carnage and place one foot in front of the next and think of walking hapless along some soft-trodden way, furry reeds underfoot, or a lush flooring of marula leaves, the smooth wind across his brow, caressing his soul in muffled whispers.

This escapism cannot last long. The group grow easily impatient with him now. If he veers off-track they yank the rope and whoever is leading him turns and yells or else comes close to him and thumps him on the top of his head or punches his shoulder. It's a rude awakening. Then the reason for crossing the wasteland becomes apparent. On the far end of the shanty, quite some distance from the remains of the shacks, there is a narrow path that opens out from a dense swagger of bush and leads them round to a small series of huts. They have not been destroyed entirely though the thatching of one has caught ablaze and collapsed into ash. They make their way to the end hut and stop. It's partially shaded by a tall wilting msasa, its dry mottled leaves have scattered a carpet across the pale dirt. The man circles the hut and looks about with some concentration. There is not another being for miles and the man is sure of this, but isn't taking any chances.

He signals for the boys to come towards him and together they start jumping up and down. It is not the end of the journey. They are not jubilant, nor have they cracked and gone mad. Their jumping is mechanical, stiff, pragmatic. After each jump they stop and move a step to one side and then jump again. After five or so jumps there is a metallic thud that booms out from beneath them. Something hollow, something cavernous beneath them sounds that strident note. They stop and drop to their knees and claw at the dust. A great russet swell plumes the air from their furrowing. They scoop off the top layer of gravel and squat next to a rectangular strip of metal sheeting nailed to what seems to be the frame of a door. They heave and push it aside and a dark, dusty cavity opens on them like the restive darkness of some tomb. The boys drop themselves down and burrow in this pit. All he can see is the swells of red dust rising and dissolving. Soon there is the sound of metal against metal. A shaft of iron points out to the sky. The man grabs it and brings it out fully into the hot shiny day, smoothing off the dust with his shirt. He stands there looking down on the weapon cradled in his arms.

The sight of the gun draws all eyes to its stiff metallic bearing, the caveat of the barrel. An automatic rifle. An AK47. Across them all echoes the splintering silence of such an unearthing. There is a stilled shudder hardening against the hotness of the day, as if none of them seems certain how to bear up in the presence of a gun. The boys feed out the beads of ammunition. Two belts in total. Hardly an arsenal to gloat about.

They pick themselves up from the pit, dust themselves off and pull the metal grid across the cavity. With their feet they rake waves of gravel over the entire enclosure. Just the bare blanketed ground now. Just a man and a gun, belts of bullets.

They gather themselves together and without a word between them they trundle on, back the way they came. The threadbare path, the ash-soaked shanties, the carious fields. This time their track is easier to traverse but the sights are no less scaring. When they veer towards the puckered roads of the outer suburbs they digress across a forking channel of paths and here the cart occasionally gets wedged between the flange of narrow bush and it's a struggle to pull it through. He strains and stamps ahead and the cab surfs through a sea of falling vlei and the woman clutches on. When he peers back he sees her scrunched grimacing face, though he doesn't hear her wail.

They diverge sharply from their path and progress northwards through the tussled bush toward another line of huts, their kerbs puddled with clay, thatched and arched in a semi-circular clearing of pale, cracked earth. The huts stand unscathed but seem deserted. The same stillness levitates over them, the same quivered fright. They stop at a hut in the middle. Its entrance is bordered with bones hanging from plaited shoots of grass attached to the jamb. There is a wooden stool placed at the entrance of the door, the wavy grain of its seat top polished to a smooth glow, its sides puckered with deep vermiculate borings. There are pots and skins and cleavers scattered about.

Inside the hut a mustiness settles over everything and beyond it the smell of crushed herbs, ground bone and blood. The bare feet of an old man are just visible, the crisp skin of his calves veined and creased and almost white in the wash of sun which licks over them. Then the figure of a small boy comes through the door gripping a spear which he flails and pegs to the hard ground before them. The boy disappears into the darkness as if he'd never been present. Just the spear dowelled to the turf. The old pair of feet haven't moved an inch.

From their group the man calls out and drops to his knees and the boys behind him drop to their knees too. His calling trails into a tune he hums or incants. He moves towards the cart and fumbles in the sacks, pulling out a packet of soya chunks and a 750 ml bottle of vegetable oil. He crawls over to place these offerings before the spear. They wait a long time before the small boy appears and in a single movement he withdraws the spear, scoops up the offerings and backs into the hut again. After a while there is the sound of a rattle stirring from the cavity. The boy emerges, the spear held out, and behind him, with a hand on the youth's shoulder, the stooping figure of an old man, his eyes sunken in his shrivelled face, pale blue, milked over, unseeing. He has a gourd in his hand, which he shakes in a perpetual dirge and across his chest is a velvety leopard pelt. He wears faded blue denims ragged at the knees.

When the old man speaks he spits as he has no teeth, just tiny pins where teeth once were. His whole face curls into the cavity of his mouth. He stands unsteadily on his feet, his hand gripping the boy's shoulder, his guide, his support. The sage talks and as he does the boy draws lines on the ground with the tip of the spear. Lines indistinguishable to anyone but those well versed in bush lore. The man looks down with deep scrutiny, listening, training his eyes on every angle, every line the boy carves. The wise man does not point but the boy points for him: a direction southwards and he animates with his hand certain things his mentor says.

Then the rattle starts up again. The boy turns, the wise man turning after him and the pair trail off slowly back inside their hut, the map he has drawn on the ground erased with a single swash of his foot across the dust.

They pick their way deep into that broad sink of land and eventually the smell of the burning and the stench of the dead is lost to the sweet waft of the fields. The city sprawl is soon screened behind by the tall ridges of bush. The lone broadcasting towers and the tall buildings fade gradually from sight as if their candescence was only temporal, faded now into some hazy oblivion of existence. No one else may ever look on them. Some clearings are low and open and only random clomps of scrub clutch at the hard, cracking turf. Here the cart and he sail along with little in the way of obstacles to deter them. The luxury of a wide berth either side, the way ahead open to them.

At other times the path narrows. The bush sprouts and thickens and staggers over them, hemming them in and then it's almost impossible to know what predators, man or beast, stalk them from the webby camouflage of the veld. But they encounter no one. Not a sound breaks from the outback. Just their thumping along. Just the rickety yammering of the cart wheels.

He has no notion where they are headed and no understanding of the scale of the journey ahead. It has taken them almost an entire day of the earth's good sun and they are barely a few miles out of the forsaken city. He hauls the woman along and she gets shunted back and forth, her tender, ripe body bashed and blasted. Still they press onwards into the unknown.

It's getting hotter and hotter. The sun's scorching rays spool over him in unfailing flashes, each one more prying, more sapping. His shoulders are knotted in balls of clay where the harness straddles him. His flesh is chaffed and goitred by now, he is sure. The rope they drag him by is ever taut and repressive. He feels as if he can't breathe at times; his mouth is numb, the gag is utterly deplorable but there is no taste now that would summon any vile reaction. It is past that. Instead the whole thing sits there across his teeth, a nebulous sheath, its filth and fetor having drained onto his tongue and dripped down his throat, dissolved there into him. His eyes are sore and sting with the sun's glare, the ever wavering gusts of dust. His back is stiff, strained, smarting. Such a catalogue of woes and they would be never ceasing if it wasn't for the fact that each foot onwards atop the crusty malm is at least a step towards some end point in this intolerable saga.

He kneads his discomforts into some general malaise and the sun overhead belts down regardless. They inch ahead, stopping occasionally for a blotch of shade under a scraggy tree where they drop to their haunches or squat against the trunk or stand doubled over to catch their breath. The woman is helped off the cart and she wobbles over to some sacks they bundle for her on the ground. No room for him under the steamy shade. He stands looking on. They carefully angle the container, trickle out some water into a Coke bottle and pass it round, sipping modestly. He begins to get agitated. The very sight of the water drives him insane. He shakes his head and moans and eventually one of the boys comes over to him and undoes the gag and raises the bottle to dribble some drops onto his expectant tongue. Each globule explodes over his flesh and kindles a thousand shudders of relief in his parched mouth.

The path ahead is blocked by a body strewn on its back, its rigid arms composed around its head, the pose of a statue knocked over on the ground. There is some noble antiquity about its demeanour that doesn't plunge their guts this time. The guise of a warrior god dumped here in its loamy tomb. Flies have flown in and are busy sucking at its opaque marbled eyes with their proboscises and as the boys are ordered in to shift its bulk their rustling wings pester the solemness of the air. The boys are quick about their business and dump the body further afield, withdrawing expressionless from the bush. A sad indictment sits over them now. So soon these horrors are absorbed, the brute indifference of a death. They strain ahead.

The ball of sun finally begins to fall out of the distant sky. The spattering ledges of clouds that had until then been bleached spumes faint across that epidemic screen. Soon, they glister purple and red and stand out like scars against the oozing cosmos. As the light dips and darkens, their raggedy shadows begin to reel against the veld bush and the scabby marl, diluting painlessly into this vast sweep of dusk light across the land. At any moment now he will raise his weary eyes to the formless horizon, and maybe somewhere he will see the first glimpse of a night-time star that will guide them onwards.

Still no stopping. Not yet is he spared the toil of it. They buckle down through the enveloping darkness and grope along their singular path. A sudden implosion of mosquitoes darts in feverishly, driving him to quick distraction with their constant droning. They are all victims; the others slap and curse, faltering in the darkening light, but he just walks on, too tired and too tied up to fend off the invasion. Small flying beetles dart into him, bouncing off and falling to the soil defeated. Some drill in his ears or claw against his body. He shakes his head to dislodge those phantom voices, but is unsuccessful.

The coolness of nightfall is a tonic, a languid spill across his weary muscles and bones: the vast exhalation of his entire being. In the next clearing they come to a halt. They look around and at one another and then the man signals the boys to dump their loads and to help the woman off the cart. They support her under the arms as she limps off clutching her bulbous stomach and whimpering, brushing tears from her cheeks. The trauma of the day has finally broken on her. The man ignores her, muttering instructions to the boys who mope about. In time the cart is unhooked and an inestimable weight falls from him. He stands there panting hard and feeling sick from the pain and exhaustion.

They rummage about for kindling and just before the full fall of night they knock together a pyre, screw strips of old newspaper into balls and strike a single match which flares the fire into crisp jagged flames. Soon the woman is crouched over dangling skewered maize cobs above the smoky heat. They gnaw sullenly, one cob each. They pass the Coke bottle round and sip at the water. He looks on and finally one of the boys comes over, undoes the gag and shunts him to the side of the clearing to allow him to feed. He drops his head and scoffs his lot. It has been a long day.

They tie him to a tree for the night but make one concession and remove the gag. Gradually the numbness in his mouth retreats and he keeps it open, lapping at the ambrosial night air to allow the coolness to salivate his raw rubbery tongue. The group is quickly asleep, curled up on sacks, rags, card, newspaper. The fire pit has been sanded over so the mosquitoes relish them all. He is too tired to fend them off, too tired to contemplate that perhaps tonight he might worm his way out of the ropes that bind him and slip off unseen into the wilderness. There is a strong smell of peat nearby – stiff, rich, reeking – and perhaps there is a shanty or a village close by. He lies there tied to the tree and nurses the pain in his back as best he can. Soon a fuzziness takes hold of his vision and a light ache inches its way up though his skull and lodges behind his eyes. He lowers his head to the chalky turf and somehow, unfathomably, he drifts off.

A gravelly hissing burrows its way into his resting thoughts and levitates there, waning and then levelling out to a high continuous bleep. His droopy sun-sore eyes quiver in response and he raises his head to see the man's hunched back towards him. He is crouched over the radio, thumbing the knob, angling the aerial at the iron blueness of the skyline. The boys are curled on the sacks. He cannot see the woman. The man sways backwards and forwards on the balls of his feet, his head moving with him as if he is meditating or working himself into a trance. There is nothing but a line of hissing, bleeping, squawking. He slaps the receiver impatiently, its frequency drops and blares but he cannot pluck the sound of the spoken word from those static, impervious airwaves. It is as if the whole world has gone silent; as if everyone has just crept away from them and curled up in a ball somewhere. He turns the knob until it clicks and is quiet suddenly. Laying the receiver on the ground, he continues to rock on his heels and look around him at the still void of night.

After this no sound sullies his sleep. The distant quake of dreams dims in some distant palpability. He sleeps for the most part, undeterred by the openness about him; the feeling of vul-nerability; the nerve chill of the militias swooping up on them from their camps in the bush and slitting their throats. Such fears only nudge the outer periphery of his mind now and then, ebbing and flowing. Once or twice he may hear footsteps across the grasses but when he opens his muggy eyes, all about him is still. The calmness of the night-time terrain. Every resting thing. At times there is just the whine of mosquitoes and at other times the sound of indefatigable beetles darting.

He dozes off and later glimpses the sight of the woman limping into the sparse scrub; squatting down, clawing her baggy dress about her waist and spewing jets of urine at the foaming earth. The sound gushes at his hazy mind. Then a leaky silence. She drops her dress and lumbers up and moves gingerly back to her repose. When he wakes again the air has greyed and warmed, the mosquitoes have vanished and there is a sweet smell of wetness leavened on the ground. The blades of grass are licked with dew. Their spiky definitions sharpen in the coming light.

The others are up and rustling about the sacks and bags. The boys pick in the bush for kindling. Soon the fire is ablaze and the woman is kneeled over it with more maize cobs. They sit huddled round the gritty hearth, each with a look of bleak resignation. Though their eyes are resolved to the slog ahead, their minds have not forgotten the pains of yesterday. They consume the meal in silence, then sand over the fire and restack the bags and sacks. The boys wheel over the cart and attach the harness to his tight stiff shoulders. They reattach the gag, which inches down across his teeth and eases against his tongue. They set off with the cool morning air coalescing about their bodies. In the distance the renascent sun stokes the sky and it turns and furls in its immensity, flushing a brief spree of puce before the pure blueness of day itself.

Then they are moiling hard, the early heat fanning down on them in this never-ceasing plain, out over the monotonous silence of the bush. The cart seems heavier this morning. The woman is still her grim self. She barely makes a sound now and her face is a waxen effigy of some stricken abhorrence. The man is strapped with the rifle, the belts of bullets like fat fingers wedged in a knuckleduster. The gun stirs a fear in his belly that does not subside. The lanky spurning boys walk on beside them. The sacks strung to their backs seem no small burden today. There is a strange dynamic to the convoy, some permanent absurdity that will never be quelled. All this and they keep walking, walking. They walk all morning and they do not see another living thing, no birds or mammals or snakes sprawled in the fanning heat.

They walk for long hours. The sun trails them from above, a sterile eye behind a microscope. The muffling bush gathers up the heat of the day and discharges it at them in some cruel osmosis. There is no breeze. The sky is still and evasive. There is not even cloud stacked across the far spheres; just a gauzy scrim and the seeming nothingness between it and the unfaltering ground they trek. It seems to them there has never been such a vastness between two points on a map. There is delirium in the air, some risen doubt. This path must lead to somewhere that is a place, to somewhere that is an end result to their labours, to something that is a release of the pain. It must lead somewhere.

The mind plays tricks. It speaks in riddles and suggests they may not have even travelled a tenth of what their aching limbs tell them. Pulling the cart is slow and tedious and draining. When its wheels jar on the unlevelled land and it can't be shunted by him alone they have to crawl to a stop yet again. The men all heave and lift and he goes charging forward to break them free from the rut. It takes some time away from the whole unending schlep of it. Then they have to stop for a snatch of shade and a rest. The woman has to dislodge and weave off into the bush to relieve herself frequently, such is the brutal bashing her bladder suffers with the weight bearing down on it. The squat chassis is blunt underneath her. The babe kicks away in a tirade of unease. At these intervals they tip the container and slosh a bit of tepid water into the Coke bottle and pass it round; all this under the steamy heat. It is quite likely after all that they have only covered some twenty or so miles.

Sometime in the early afternoon they come to a village, which resembles a wasteland burnt flat to the ground by some apoca-lyptic scourge no one has told the world of: a place sanitized by burning. They are weary. The boys are sent ahead to survey the area, their machetes raised. Bit by bit they creep forward towards its charred circumference, akin to a space scorched deep on the ground by a rocket launch. So intense has the inferno been here that there is nothing distinguishable beneath the black clumps of debris, the sagged mulch of melted things that have fallen to this slurry pit. All is soot and ash and a splay of blackness which shifts in sheets off the periodic breeze. Even the bones that lie here half buried within it are sure to be charred, glazed and incendiarized.

There is nothing of value that they can scrape up from this pit – the fields are already plundered of their scabby crops, the livestock wired up and yoked and hauled away – so they make a cursory inspection of its perimeter and then move on. Such an episode scores itself tangibly into the still whiteness of the coming afternoon hours and for a while afterwards they all feel drenched in a fine crust of slag, those last finite remnants clinging to them. They walk for a long time and do not come across another such village that day.

It is just the veld they plunge into and it is so thick it could well be virgin bush that parts its arched walls and opens up its tunnel to them as they press ever forward. Its stooping hood is staggered over them; growth that no eye can penetrate. There may be swags of trees festooned out in the vastness of this beige sea, their tasselled tips frothed like surf, but their struggle is in vain; they are swamped and sunk. Only the path cuts through it, trodden threadbare and compacted smooth beneath them like a slip of balding skin.

Along the path there are other paths: the turf has splintered and webbed into a network of crevices that open up in miniature cavities. Here ants and termites may nest but they are seldom to be seen. They may be down there in those cool recesses. They may be hidden away from the foot of man. Or perhaps they are already attuned to the perils of the path.

When in the late afternoon the sun's eye finally breaks its concentrated stare and begins to droop into the far corners of the horizon, the light blurs and smirches the tufted tops of the rooi grass and their red inflorescence is lost in a blink. He has lost track of time and its beady accentuation of his plight. Each step of the day pulling the cart is a mark of some penance served. Some penance or sacrament he has no knowledge of. He has just been walking and the cart has lumbered on behind him in his shadow and mounted in her cab the woman has, like him, dropped off mindlessly and lost the hours. He hasn't heard a sound for some time that isn't the grating whine of the wheels slurping against the axle. Even this has become at one with the forbidding silence of their progression, the stilled land that stands mute as their creaking presence rolls over it like an unwelcome heathen skulking across the town square to the vaulted doors of a church.

At the man's command, they come to an unexpected halt. There is little space on the path to rest and recline. The man mutters to the boys and they drop their sacks and move to the back of the cart and stand over the woman who reclines in her barge as a queen attended by her eunuchs. If they had palm fronds they may have fanned her flushed and sleeted face. The man has gone. He has crept away ahead of them all along the path and they must wait for his return.

He is gone for a while. The tired boys drop to the ground and sit, resting against the cart. They may fall asleep. Occasionally they swipe at flies that zoom in on them in their prime stillness and feast and suckle the sweat on them. He cannot lie or rest and so must stand there laboured with the weight of the cart on his back. His legs ache in spasms. The pain is centred at the very pith of his bones and it quivers outwards criss-crossing the fibres of his flesh. His back is stiff, his shoulders throb. Where the ropes bind him he is chaffed and tender; it may not be long till the skin breaks and the ropes dig into his thinning blades, scouring flush against the bone.

When the man comes back the boys try to get to their feet but they are too slow. He has caught them at their sloth. He dives on them from above in a spurt of rage. He pegs one of them to the turf and stands over him kicking the point of his shoe into the boy's ribs as he squeals in a half-broken voice and tries in vain to fend off the blows. The gun swivels from his shoulder and the belts of bullets flap a rhythm against his hips. The man breaks off and turns on the other boy in a flash, slapping him about his head and yelling and pushing him till he keels into the bushes. The woman's screams increase until he yells in her face, raising his hand above her. She cowers and stiffens, swallowing her cries in a gulp of fear.

There is relative silence now. The stifled breaths, the muted whimpering. The man stands back, breathing hard and looking down on their failings as a father does who knows the stack of his unsung sacrifices. The kneeling boys look up at him like dogs scorned by their master. Then all is broken. The man sulks away and scoops up the rope and pulls him on and he staggers forward, the cart wobbling onwards; the boys pick themselves up and limp after.

They move along the path for a good half hour before they stop again. The man raises his hand to silence and still them. He stands looking ahead, knowing well that the eye can't see through the pall of bush. He drops the rope, lowers himself to his haunches and not for an instant does he break his stare. He signals to the boys and in unison they drop to the ground too, squatting over the low spiky tufts of the glimmering scrub grass. Here they wait, hushed, inhaled, hidden.

There is the threat that even a single breath stolen from this inimical air will warn some stooping unseen foe of their presence. The air has thickened, furling overhead in an elastic splay of tension. Twisted and muscled and knotted. Off to the side of him he alone can observe the last struggling arcs of the raddled sun slipping under the fuzzed surface of the horizon, sinking like a vessel ablaze after some drawn, unconscionable wrecking. Then a grim iron gloaming shudders across the sky in its dying moments, hanging nebulous and bleary before the fullness of night.

The man has been sitting cross-legged at their helm, staring into the impervious screen that is shunted ahead of them. The boys, too, are sat on the dust of the path, their sacks beside them each balanced on the scrub. They wait patiently and don't dare render up a moment of their tiredness or boredom. They nurse their wounds in silence. Saddled in the middle is the woman reclined in her tub. She has not made a sound in ages nor moved a muscle. Perhaps she has even slipped away into a world of the unconscious where the full extent of her indifference can be borne. He can only stand there harnessed to the cart; as much as he would like to he can't hunker down and lay his body across the coolness of the threadbare path, spreading his aching tendons and dipping his throbbing bones into the soothing emollient of the earth. He must stand there and wait.

When at last the man is convinced that the night is at its deepest, he crawls from his post to the cart and fiddles silently with one of the sacks. His face is inscribed with some deep concentration, a fixed, determined stare. He draws out a reel of steel wire and unravels a length in his hands, feeding it into a thin groove on the iron frame of the cart, working it as a blacksmith may until the piece wears through and weakens, coming away clean from the coil. He must have a good metre stretched in his hands. He deposits the reel back in the sack and creeps along the path without a word. The boys strain and look on, but within seconds his body has slipped into the dark tunnel of the path and has been enveloped by the seeming nothingness beyond it.

They wait there for what seems a painful passing of time. He can no longer bear the strain and finally begins to shuffle on his feet, pulling against the harness, feeling the fullness of the weight of the cart like a lead sarcophagus behind him. At once the boys are at his side and one of the machetes is raised and angled at his neck, though it means nothing to him now. The other boy is behind him and punches his hip to stop him from scuffling on his feet. He feels his midriff splice through with a pain that quakes his very innards. He can barely stay upright, but the boys have him at the harness, holding him up. He tries to struggle free and snap his head at them but the gag is tight and wedged firm into his mouth, paralyzing him. In their grip he cannot lash out and overpower them so they stand there rather absurdly, the three of them, jostling silently amongst themselves as if they were all small children squabbling over a toffee apple.

Then through the slim darkness the man runs towards them. The boys drop their grip and stagger back. The man repeats something in a breathless, urgent rant and the boys jump into action, scurrying for their sacks. The man picks up the dangling rope and pulls on it with a violent jerk. It shunts his neck and he almost trips in his precarious balance. He groans through the gag, straining against the rope out of some primitive protest. He tries to dig his heels into the turf and recoil his whole body from the force that pulls on him, the prepotent tension. The man tugs, yanking at him but as tired as his legs are he manages to grip his heels against the earth and hold his course. His stubbornness comes from some sudden welled loathing. His captor is beginning to panic. He can sense his advantage over this man who keeps looking ahead at the path he has just returned from, pulling at him with a desperate urgency. He calls to the boys and they come swooping in and push him from behind. His weight topples forward and he is forced to give up his stand. The cart edges along. All the while the woman lies there, her expressionless face screened from the mayhem.

The man leads them with haste along the path. The wheels of the cart slip along the cooling earth, the chassis wobbling in waves from side to side – it has perhaps never managed speeds like this before. They are almost at a canter. Their quickening breaths are fuming the air, curling back on their flushed faces. The man mumbles something incessantly – he may well be talking to himself or he may be urging them on. The others don't seem to react either way but just press along with their sacks strewn over their shoulders and their raspy breathing grunting all the while. Soon they come to a sudden clearing. The man halts and raises his hand and they all come to a sharp stop behind him. Like cartoon characters they could well have rammed into the back of him. The man paces and looks right and left. He beckons and the boys come forward, pulling him. They cross a short levelling of stony ground and weedy shrubs and then the path dips through an incline that's as deep as a ditch. He struggles to ascend it. The belly of the cart wedges itself briefly in the cupped hollow but the boys are behind it at once, heaving it up and onwards, pushing while he staggers ahead.

On the other side, they find themselves on the edge of a wide tarred road. It looks like the miracle of some unearthing, some lost and ancient place. The stretch of asphalt grey and granular, long like a lick of tongue. On either side of the road there are two petrol drums painted in white and grey stripes. A wooden log runs atop them in a beam. The man hurries them on and they step onto the road, then edge onto the stony clearing and trail down into the ditch, re-entering the hooded tunnel of the path.

Lying there in the trench as they pass they do not see the two slender strips of mottled camouflage, warm and still, posited there in their ready-made graves. They have been hauled limp and lifeless across the tarmac, each one taken from the tedious silences of their dreary watch, and the corners of the heels of their boots may be glassed over with the powdery whiteness of attrition. Otherwise they look asleep; hardly touched or throttled. The swelling at their throats is insignificant. One of them still has the coil of wire wrapped tight round his windpipe.

They carry on a good distance in the dark. After a while they ease into their step again. The boys slouch along with the weight of the sacks bearing down on them. The woman is awake now – he can hear her wistful sighs behind him, the occasional deep-bellied groan that cracks on the back of the stiff night air. The cart wheels climb over the skewered tracks and then thump down into the recesses. The wheels slam against the frame and send a hammering through her numb and prickly rump. It has been a long day. She has had enough.

At the front the man leads on, the freakish fifth limb of his rifle flat against his back and protruding above his head. He seems determined to get them as far away from the road as possible. Perhaps cast jaggedly across his quiet demeanour is the quaking heart that beats in his chest like a drum. Its off-beat racing rhythm is pivoted at the moment he flexed the wire in his hands and took a deep breath and slipped from the roadside bushes, a bodiless force towards the first of his lazing victims. How he managed to pull it off only he can ever know.

They walk so far into the night each step becomes nothing but a mechanical placement on some ever revolving treadmill. The scene never changes. Tall staggered shards of bush encumber them. It may well be a painted backdrop awash with long blotchy strokes which they troop in front of in a pantomime scene. Or it could now be the far somnambulism of the mind. Some ether where they tread on vapours and the cool air sings some hymn of emancipation.

Finally a glade opens up to the left of them. The man staggers into it and stops and looks about. He signals to the boys. They drop to their knees and an audible sigh from them all breaks into the soft openness of this place. They sit, heaving and sucking in air as if they have at last crossed the tape at the end of a marathon. Attached to the cart, he must stand and endure the torture a while longer.

Later they are curled on the sacks and cardboard, dead to the world. They finally got round to unbinding the ropes and loosening the gag and wheeling away the cart. He staggered on his feet; the relief was pulverizing. He scoffed his food and drank the water they spared him and was content to be led into the low grasses and tied to the thin pole of a tree. His legs collapsed from under him and he lay there against the trunk, his mind already blanking as he drew his head to rest.

When he wakes the full sun is up and wood smoke drifts towards him, settling in his nostrils and stoking his brain to consciousness. The woman is hunched over the pyre turning skewered maize cobs in the rounds of her stubby swollen fingers. She looks sullen, her lips downcast and drawn, her eyes marbled with some distant dappling of despair. The boys perch by her close as puppies, waiting for the bony maize stalks to brown, char and soften.

The man sits hunched on his feet drawing lines in the soil with a stick. Some personal cartography. He is preoccupied, lost in his own imaginings, his own calculations. He whispers to himself. He closes his eyes, mutters, draws deep into the well of his memory. He opens his eyes again and counts on his digits and scrawls in the dust. Then he turns to a jagged cutting of card and scribbles something with the blackened tip of a twig cooling now like the greying filament of a poker rod. After breakfast and water they reset the gag, wrap the ropes about his shoulders and wheel round the cart. And so another day becomes them all.

They mope along. Well past noon the woman finally breaks the static silence and curls into a heaving mass of hysteria. Low rising cries at first and then she bawls a wrenching tirade. She clubs her fists against the sides of the cab and screams, crying as if she were giving witness to some revelation scored in the sky. The man tries to snatch her wrists but she lashes out at him. She scratches at the air like the victim of a swarm. The boys rush to her and they all grip her arms and steady her swipes and try to mute her screaming. She struggles under their arrest. Finally they lift her from the cart and drag her into the bush. He hears a sharp slap and then her steady whimpering behind the khaki veil of the grass. Her gibbered plangencies surrender to a steady hiss of sobs and pleading.

There is nothing and no one about. The snaking path lies open ahead. He stands listening. They come staggering out of the bush and plop her back into the cart. Stern words are uttered at her. The man scolds the boys and mutters angrily to himself as if everything is a conspiracy against him, against his vast deplorable scheme. He is still murmuring when he walks in front of the cart and hits him across the back of the scalp and his mind dims to the blow, his vision swimming but he finds he is walking on regardless.

She hunches down in the cab, silent and sulking. Her master stoops on, a thrawn stoic begrudging his obligations. They trundle through an unravelling sameness of place. Nothing has ever changed in this world of soil and grass and sky. It is like something elemental stabbed on a frieze, on a slip of canvas, its infinite permanence hewed at the beginning of time and forgotten. The taut afternoon air suckles on their bodies and shadows the distemper of the group. Five forlorn beings it has made of them. Deep in that landscape there is a path that leads onwards to some distant purpose; forged and weathered by the feet of time.

Still they nudge on. Their weary limbs; their downcast moods; the pester of the errant flies that come sometimes and at other times are wholly conspicuous by their absence. They walk and stop and rest to measure out a dram of water into the Coke bottle and reward themselves the relief of it, an elixir measured on the tongue as if in pitiless spoonfuls. Then they put away the bottle, screw the lid tight on the water container, and walk on again.

They are perhaps only fifty miles away from the city. How can they tell? How can the tiredness of the feet and the aches in the limbs measure distance? Maybe they had travelled seventy miles, their collective minds dulled into weary submissiveness. All that toil and only this meagre smattering of distance to show for it.

Deeper and deeper into the heart of the country they go and with each passing step their minds get lost to the unfathomable terrain they travel, the delusions it conjures. They stay clear of main roads. They bypass all the little dorps that are dotted along them, if the dorps are not all levelled to rubble, brick, ash, burnt beyond all recognition. They skirt road signs, if there are road signs left to tell them anything, if their iron poles are not yet yanked from the ground and carted off and smelted down. They sidestep all the compass points they may have known; the familiar assurances of the road, the chartered course. Instead they plunge the forbidding trails of bushmen and peasant farmers and rural dwellers, the man always stopping them to consult his scrap of card and screening back in his mind to the fast-fading words of the wise man. But it leads to nothing at all that is certain in the mind. No placement of the foot along the path that is anything but a thumb suck in the vacant wind.

The day passes in a haze of heat and bleached bush and the silences of this hermitic land. Noon comes awash on the consciousness and in the hours afterwards, memory swims beneath the skull and only surfaces to acknowledge the occasional dim sting of a lashing they issue him when he stumbles from his path. Only later in the afternoon when the sun at last curves away does he re-emerge to the tedium of the day now racked up against him, the tension so great it feels as if his brain may pop. Then he would be just a dazed stream of simplicity; his body and the cart plodding along until finally the twitching nerves realized their fate and the whole contraption fell to a great heap in the bush.

A t last the dusk air thickens before his nose, grey against the metallic horizon. They walk and walk. All day this crawl across hard soils. An aimless journey. Rocks against which his feet succumb to numbness and stones to which his skin is hopelessly reconciled. There is little to hurt him by now. Thorns of the scrub are no longer vehement. Spiky branches part before his chest so easily it's as if he is wading through water, plunging the mystic depths. His body is a vessel. Of what he does not know. His mind is sun battered and his brain is shrivelled to nothingness beneath his crisp scalp. His head is just a shell during this unending trudging and the heat of these daylight hours. A space within a space where if one stopped him and pressed their ear to his ear they would possibly hear the ocean there. The wavy lapping hollowness breaking in primal rhythms on a blonde shore.

They may walk like this for many hours and many days and still not stumble across another village or kraal or being. They may walk one whole day of this unending solitude and then be tricked at the end of it to assume they have travelled more. So easily the heat dapples with the mind and its convictions. Such is the drag of the foot upon the rutted turf, the clomping assimilation of distance, the sense of disorientation now scoured into them. Some force in the air is sucking the sanity from them little by little, minute by minute as each lone second passes.

The woman lies in the clutch of the trap he drags her in. Her legs are splayed immodestly over the sides and she is hunkered down there on sparse rags and bedding, the sacks and container between her thighs. She is inert, sometimes like a mannequin, something to be plopped down between the clutter or folded away. Her gaunt face, her tightened mouth grinning inanely at the vapid air. Her bulging stomach rises from her bony torso, a pocket of fluid in which her child flicks about like a fish in its confinement, its lungs filled with waters from the deepest of seas and plumbed from the most endless, the most unfathomable darkness. Pooling and pooling into the essence of existence. Here it flashes about, it flinches. But it may never surface into this realm of the living.

She grows ever more despondent. Sometimes she is completely unresponsive and her body lies there in a static heap whilst she has slipped down into the depths of some catatonic moroseness. She is no virago. When they stop now it sometimes takes all three of them to ease her out of the cab and carry her off into the bush where she slumps on her haunches and does her business and is carried back stinking of shit and crying feverishly. Sometimes she hoists herself up on her arms and vomits over the side of the cart and its aftermath dribbles down her chin and settles in the hollow of her neck, drying there, crisp, in the sun.

The man loses his patience and doesn't heed to her heaving or hurling. The boys try to rig up a canopy of some sticks wired to the cart and an awning of sack stretched across a rickety frame to shelter her. She slumps down completely in its mottled shade and is lost even further to the world. They don't hear a sound from her for hours until the wheels get rammed on a ledge or a protruding root and the canopy comes swooping down on her and she wakes with a shudder, whining and wailing, clutching her gut.

As for him, his back hurts more and more from lugging the load behind him. His captive's dues. His spine aches with stiffness. The thing is so unwieldy, so infirm, so unbalanced that he has not been able to grow accustomed to it. He should become used to walking how he has to walk nowadays, carting this burden behind him. There ought to be a sense of balance in his posture or a levelling out of weight distribution. The load should by now be absorbed into his own weight and his own body; becoming one with him. But he can never get used to it. Things no longer make sense. Out here, in this world.

So the pain is always there sunk like a coldness into his bones and there is no respite for it, not even in sleep. Sometimes he thinks he dozes off while walking. His legs just keep trundling, spokes in a machine, and his mind becomes dulled to the whipping they issue if he slows down or veers off-course. At least his captors have no option but to realize he serves them little purpose if his legs buckle and he drops in the vlei dead or stumbles off the edge of a kopje. If he goes down what will become of the woman and the child in her belly? Here perhaps there is a certain degree of leverage between himself and them, so at last they do stop for a while. They give him a gulp of water, momentarily relaxing the rope bound round him, knowing he won't run because he would rather have the water brought to his lips instead.

But every day there eventually comes a point when the sun plummets red into the dust-filled distance and in the strip between the black haze of seething earth and the furling blueness of sky something kindles there which may just be the first inkling of nightfall. How much longer? How much more plodding along this unnerving path before some gift of respite? The grey air thickens. The strip of night widens.

When the heat wave dips entirely he surfaces from his shrunken malaise of isolation and begins to detect slow shifts in the rhythm of travel, sloth in the motions of the group. He knows soon they will think about resting and start to look for a place to stop. His eyes are sunshot but he will still be able to see the grey stalking figures of the group ahead in the duskfall. He will be able to see them halt and scan the orange flush for promising campsite locations. They will mutter to one another, standing there contemplating the bush, the tense electric air.

When they do settle down for the night it's at some makeshift campsite. A clearing or a cave if they are lucky to find one. They come to a halt and he stands and watches as they unravel their back packs and rummage in the sacks and spread their wares. They do not command his assistance in this. The woman of the daytime and the evening are two separate people. She suddenly comes alive in the absence of the sun. Or she is simply energized by a sense of duty or guilt. She clambers off her perch in the cart and stretches her aching spine and peels back the sacks. She deals out a cup of mealie-meal or skins four small figs. The boys mope about collecting kindling for the fire. The wood is dry and the grass burns easily; it is no great effort. The mealie-meal she steams in a cutting of sack because they cannot afford to squander the water on boiling it. It comes out like wedged slabs of clay they mould in their fingers and bury the figs in. Or else she cooks it a while longer till it looks close to chinks of slate, hard colourless cakes that snap in the hand, sometimes disintegrate.

They make no attempt to wash or attend well to their toilet. In the end the reek of stale odours grows into a musty fogginess and is forgotten and forgiven by the wild. It matters little out here. The men stop and turn aside and piss the little water their bodies hold out at the glinting stalks of grass. He is the same. Or else they reel into the bush or round a tree and squat and defecate, the waste dropping from their emaciated torsos with grim reluctance. If the wind should pick up at night it carries the stiffness of their stools wafting back towards them but otherwise it is lost in the expanses forever.

They bed down on blankets and rags and are able to drift off as if it were the most natural thing in the world. They make a bonfire which can only be to ward off the notion that a pack of hyenas may sniff them out or a leopard may be crouched in the trees above them as they hardly ever sit about it and commune. They're too tired and so they drop off soon after. Predators of the wild never come. There probably isn't an animal left native to these parts that isn't already a stiff shell bedded in the ground, its flesh scraped clean by poachers.

Sometimes they mutter for a while and then drop off. What they talk about, what complaints they level, what fears they share is unknown to him. Sometimes it happens that even in the midst of all this the night stirs unlikely passions. In the deep ends of a cave one night where the firelight dashed dimly off the reddened walls, she pleasured the man orally, pitying him because he can't get any while she's in her state. Or the night he knelt before her and slipped a finger into her slack cunt and stimulated her gently and the look of teetering pleasure she exuded completed her bewildering metamorphosis from the figure who writhes in pain all day in the cart to the figure who lies together with her man propped up against a rock or a tree. All this before she remembered her condition or it became uncomfortable for her to maintain such an intrusion into her burgeoning body and she stopped him.

The boys are active too. In the late darkness they sometimes wake and restively fumble at their trousers or shorts and out jut their stiff erections. They lie there jerking off until the inevitable spasm grips them. They pan the effluent whiteness into the palm of their hands or it specks the sweaty blackness of their stomachs – they are of an age where the seed is eager and flows free and fast – and then they fall at once to rest and the quickening pull of sleep.

Such voyeurism invokes no guilt. No feeling that's uncomfortable to him, no sick desire, no illicit longing. He looks on brazenly, not even registering fully what he sees, his insular mind adrift in some desperate lodging. The long lonesome nights with nothing to do. The sheer exhaustion of the day pressed over him, a hand that muffles the consciousness. Stiff and unable to get comfortable he stays awake for an inestimable time. He peers at them from across the raggedy bonfire and sees the flickers dart on their sleeping faces, the sweat-glow of contentment. If the wind picks up it grows bitterly cold and the pain eases into something akin to an icepack on his back followed by eventual numbness that is not numbness itself but another type of pain altogether. He can't win. He tries to creep as close to the fire as the rope will allow him until one of the group rouses from sleep and shouts at him or throws a stone at him to move away into the cold and the dark. At such times he could shed a tear. If he knew how to weep after all this or if it were possible, he would cry for the pity of it. He would cry for a good night's sleep, a barn of dry hay.

But he can't weep and so he nestles down there to another rest-less night chained to a tree or fixed to a biting outcrop. He cannot despise their primitiveness either: that they can lie down any-where and fall asleep in a second. The night wears on steadily enough. Occasionally the man is up and about stooping round them, the rifle clutched at the ready. But mostly all is still and quiet and just his mind is spooling.

2

12 October

Veronica came & put up a sign outside the gate today. My initial instincts: crude, tasteless, tacky. An insipid orange with that rather unimaginative logo of her agency stencilled onto it, 'For Sale' scrawled diagonally across it in a thick blue screed. So much for discretion. As soon as I saw it something in me numbed: I suppose the tangible realization that things are going ahead. Concrete steps & all that. Sixpence pegged it into the flowerbed, just beside the gate sign with the family name on it. Somehow it seemed to eradicate it, possess it. Felt as if I'd already packed up & gone.

'That'll get things ticking,' Veronica said, her customary pre-conditioned smile flashing away.

'We'll see,' I murmured.

13 October

A weary Saturday. I woke up in a downcast mood & remained in one for much of the day. A constant, irritable drizzle falling outside & the grey skies bleak & glum. The rains are v. early this year, though I still suspect the food crisis will be blamed on drought. Drought & illegal sanctions imposed by Western neo-colonizers!

Spent much of the morning reading in bed, too indolent to get up. Heard Tobias clattering about in the kitchen, then the old familiar smell of chicken casserole wafting down the passage. It rekindled in me some heady nostalgia, taking me at once to memories of my youth & the smells in the house of Mom's cooking. I didn't get up & go into the kitchen, but from bed I imagined the scene all too vividly: Tobias frying the onions & the peppers & the ginger, mixing the special sauce which comes from no cookbook, but is ingrained from years of Mom's tutoring.

I wonder if in Australia she still makes the same casserole? I wonder if the ingredients blend in the same way, whether the spices fuse as they do here in Africa? I don't suppose you can get Viljoen's All-Wors Spices in Perth. Unless Viljoen himself also left in the great migration & continues plying his trade to every home-sick African? What a clever little enterprise that would be. Come to think of it I haven't seen Viljoen's Spices in the shops since the meltdown, but that isn't so surprising.

I wonder if Mom too, smelling the whole thing baking away in the oven, is ever kindled with thoughts of Zimbabwe & this house (that was after all her mother's house) & how she taught the then green Tobias how to cook from scratch? Before any of us were born & when she & Dad were just married & taking on a house-hold of their own.

'That old munt didn't know a thing I didn't teach him,' she used to boast. 'He came to me straight from the bush.'

Yes, I wonder if she too is moved to the same pangs of longing & melancholy? If she knew how to send an e-mail I'd ask her. If the phones here were a bit more reliable I'd probably be able to tell from the tone of her voice, albeit crackled over with static noise & a five-second delay.

Later I found I wasn't hungry. Tobias took the dish from the warming drawer & proudly set it on the counter alongside a steaming bowl of rice. I looked at it & then waved him off, telling him to put it into a Tupperware dish for later. He stood there

looking stunned & bemused as if this slight signalled my dis-
pleasure with him. He said, 'What is wrong, baas?'

Of course he wouldn't know. 'Nothing,' I snapped, 'I'm just not
hungry.'

Went into the lounge & watched TV & felt low for the rest of
the night.

14 October

It must be the sign outside the gate that is putting me in this
mood. As if, somehow, that fat stake has been hammered into me,
into my skin, slicing the roots that bind me. Feel unsettled &
unsure. Have given to doubting my decision to sell up & leave. If
the truth be told I struggle to find an actual reason, to pinpoint the
moment or act that triggered off the impulse to chuck it all in. It
wasn't something very definitive that did it & this I suppose plays
on my mind.

It wasn't, for instance, another vitriolic presidential speech
blared out on the TV or hateful headlines in the state paper that
did it. I like to tell myself I'm too immune to all that after thirty-
odd years even though I know deep down it still riles my guts
each & every time. What they say to us, the way they paint us all
with the same brush because our skin is white & halfway across
the world there's an island they blame for everything where
people happen to have white skin. Just once I'd like to stand up &
tell some fat party boy that we both have common links – more,
comrade, than you'd like to think. I'd say: you who fought the
British in the bush thirty-five years ago & never let anyone forget
it, well a century ago my mother's father's father fought the
British around the kopjes of Magersfontein, had his family
rounded up into a concentration camp in Mafeking, his fields

burnt, his homestead looted. Where does that leave us now, comrade, in this strange disposition? What does that say, face to face, eye to eye? Somehow I can't see my claim being v. penetrating!

Maybe I am just contaminated by the same unplaced, nebulous infectious spirit that seems prevalent amongst many of my kinsmen? The mindset that says we deserve better than this, that for some reason greener pastures are justly deserved, a birthright of the pale skinned & that we needn't tolerate this mindless ineffectual chaos a day longer. So we sell up & pack up & dissipate ourselves far & wide where we just expect to carry on, one day to next, one country to another. That's what Mom & Dad, Alex & James did. Dad just threw up his arms when the company went under & had Mom sign the house over to me & they just took off as soon as they could get visas, severing all ties. But I am fearful of this weakness most of all. Of being the willing victim of a trendset, one of the flock, the rambling pack. But still I find myself inching along with my intentions, pulled in this wake & with no real appetite to stop myself.

When the rain stopped in the evening I decided to go for a walk around the neighbourhood. Maybe I could walk off my sullenness, so I thought. Everything was dripping in green & the trees on the pavements were heavy with water. The aroma of coolness, of damp African dust v. prominent. Down Argyle Rd, there were no less than seven houses with 'For Sale' signs up, all glinting in the late breaking sun, vying for attention. Somehow I doubt if Veronica's orange & blue effort will be able to compete.

15 October
The power went off last night. That sudden plunge into blackness is always startling. I was up late preparing notes for the lower six

when they went & for some moments I just sat there, the spools of dark gyrating around me & an instant feeling in my stomach of something I can only describe as dread. But dread at what, of what? When one is plunged into the dark the dread is instinctive, it's of the unknown, the formlessness about you, sightlessness of a known reality. Everything has gone but in a way that is only relative to you, your lack of sight. It is difficult to describe in the clear light of day now, but for a few moments then, something dreadful did come over me, something I sensed is linked to my precarious situation. I wonder if this darkness & dread embodies 1) the dire situation of this country, the abyss it's in: in a nutshell everything I'm trying to escape or 2) my own unshaped, undecided future. Perhaps everything is around me, just as it's always been, the structures & parameters of my life, just that I am presently stumbling along it in the dark unable to see the light at the end of the corridor? Well in the end I groped my way down the passage & clawed into bed, moody & embittered, though I ought to be used to this by now. The power has yet to come back. When I got home today & walked into the kitchen I could already hear the silences of the fridge & freezer. Ominous looming quiet. The water in the geyser is still tepid enough for a bath of sorts but if this carries on it'll be back to the cold water bucket & sponge. Thank God it isn't winter.

16 October

Still off. I'm not going to worry about it today. Earlier I was invited to Hedgehogs by a group of the staff, the outgoing bunch. I'm surprised they even still ask me as I usually decline at once, fumbling for some excuse, even though I often regret it later. But today I accepted without hesitation. I thought: why not?

Anything is better than the dark tedium of the house. When I got home in the evening I told Tobias to go off. He looked a little shattered. He had assembled the gas & scottle braai & was preparing to fry me a pork chop & heat some sweetcorn. I said, 'Don't worry about that, I'm going out,' & left him standing in the kitchen, no doubt looking down glumly at the braai disc.

So this is how it is to be, he probably thought, *now that the boss is selling up & heading for the horizon. Am I to be thus discarded? My efforts disdained, my loyalty brushed aside?* Already I've told him to chuck the chicken casserole from Saturday, completely untouched, as the fridge isn't holding up in this power cut.

Hedgehogs was dreary. As I was pulling up in the car park a moment of apprehension clouded over me & I had the sudden nervous thought that I'd made a mistake accepting & thinking I'd enjoy myself. Something pitted in my stomach, hard like a stone. I don't know why this happens. I can't recall when it started, so long back I don't care to remember. But something in me recoils when the prospect of contrived human contact looms. Mingling with people I hardly know & hardly care an iota for. I sat there, the car parked, the engine off & a brisk vision of the night before me rolled across my mind. All the familiar resentments & loathing. I wasn't enthused.

Didn't stay long. Had two beers & an argument with that irrepressible flirt Stacey Brisk over something intellectually trite. Seemed as good a barrier as anything I could concoct. Then as I was leaving I thought I glimpsed a familiar face at a table in the far corner. The light was dim there & I can't be sure, but I could have sworn it was Alicia Wall.

Now at home in the candlelight I'm writing this entry & wondering if it really was her. But what confounds me more is this:

why am I wondering? Why didn't I just go over to the table & if it was her, greet her? Show my pleasant surprise at her return from abroad, catch up on old times? What is it that makes me retreat so from those around me, the society that inhabits the same space as me? Why is it that I'm rather drawn to the insulation of these pages, the walls of this house where I am incubated from the outside by fragments of the past?

17 October

The power has been off for three days now. When it went I hoped it was just the usual load-shedding cut, but now I know to reconcile myself to the inevitable. Have tried to phone to report it but of course can't get through or they don't answer. The last fault lasted a month, the one before even longer. Can't bear to think how long this one's going to drag on for. The usual story I presume: no money for spare parts, no technicians to carry out repairs. Suppose you can't blame them for doing a runner if they've hardly been paid a cent for six months, can you?

I don't mind the quietness so much. I've realized this. I rather like the silence in the house, that vibe not sifting through the walls of things humming, rattling, bubbling away. A certain peaceable remoteness one gets. I can live without appliances too. That's the joy of the book, this journal, the piano. From another age where quietness reigned, where calmness presided. It's just the whole hassle of the fridges & freezers, the meat going off, the milk sour-ing, etc. And I'd just gone & stocked it up. I can ill-afford to but rumours abound of the prices going up again next week. (Funny how in Africa, in such times, even the US dollar attracts such a rate of inflation!) Someone told me that if you wrap a blanket over the freezers they keep iced for longer. May have to try it.

18 October

No change. Tired today. Before the sun slipped away (the rains seem to have abandoned us) I was reading out on the veranda & felt my eyes growing heavy. The garden is so lush this time of year. Traces of Mother's touches everywhere still, though they've been gone almost ten years already. A lot of the plants flowering now she planted herself. Cut them back in the winter & they just spring up again in summer, like some force that can't be vanquished. Something I'll certainly miss. Am trying to put all other thoughts to the back of my mind re. the move, leaving, etc. I suppose the danger is of getting lost in the escapism of a world whose landscape lies across the pages of a book. Or the deep engrossment of the mind: I have been thinking pleasurably in the dark of Alicia these last two nights, her face ingrained in my mind as I drift off, that specific scent of her effusing in my memory with astonishing ease.

19 October

I've heard nothing further from St James' College about my job application, not a word from Veronica about the house. Tonight I fired up the old genny for a few hours. Thought I'd resist longer this time but the freezers are my main concern & justification. Plus it's just so miserable once the sun sets sitting here by myself in the candlelight or the dim glow of the hurricane lamp. Tried to read by it the last few nights but got too tired too quickly. The orange glow falling over the page does it I think: too soporific. So I got Sixpence to fuel it up & ran it for a while. The house lit up like a Christmas tree. An island in this suburb of dark. I caught up with the cricket highlights on TV, watched a bit of BBC news. All the while I could hear the chug of the diesel motor outside.

Suddenly I felt an alarming guilt. Quite unquantifiable. As if the glower of lights, the blare of the TV were tantamount to a type of gluttony. This when everything has been so frugal of late! I suppose I was thinking about the fuel & how I really can't afford to squander it. So I stomped outside & turned it off. Rather embittered that I was made to feel so shameful by such an insignificant luxury as a few hours' electricity.

20 October

In the upper-six lesson I got into a spat with Edwards, something that seems to have deepened this stupor of late, not lifted it. Factors attributing to the rise of fascism, etc. All v. racy stuff, as far as the history syllabus 3108/8 goes. Mostly the boys lapped up my preamble with no real reaction, but I could detect Edwards sitting there weighing up everything with that blank, dispassionate look of his I've come to know not as arrogance but as some sort of osmosis, some kind of intellectual digestive process. Sometimes I wonder whether I'm looking at myself when younger & I marvel fondly at the similarities. I remember discussions when my teachers often thought I wasn't even present in the room & passed biting remarks about my conceited aloofness. The better ones knew of course that I was normally biding my time, processing the information before seizing the eventual moment to argue back. Sometimes I said nothing & then spilt it all in essays or papers. Sometimes Edwards does that too.

I was hoping today he'd just shut up. Truth is I haven't really felt up for a fight of late. Something about pulling a carpet of security away from under your own feet is unsettling intellectually. It's been said of me that I've wasted my time teaching a mixed bag of schoolboys the scant shallowness of A-level history when I could have carved out a promising career as a university academic, a professor, lecturing the crème de la crème at the best institutions abroad, penning scholarly texts on my field of expertise – Africa & its litany of problems. That I'm over-qualified for this job is an understatement. I just started studying one day, drawing deeper & deeper into that murky well of the past & no one told me when to stop, no one drew my head up for breath. I was left there to drown in my own notions of a bygone reality. The degrees stacked up from the correspondence university with alarming ease & time & the normal progression of life seemed to saunter by with only a passing nod.

I suppose I have no one to blame but myself. All the while this house got flooded with books, extensions of my cerebral haemorrhaging I couldn't stop & even when Mom & Dad were still here they'd complain about being overridden with bulky volumes I'd plunder cheaply from car boot sales, dusty second-hand shops, flea markets. Books on anything & everything. A house of books: a house within a house. How am I going to dismantle it? I could never afford to truck them all down to South Africa. My lodgings at St James' will probably be woefully inadequate anyway. And some yuppie upstart graduate will point out to me the virtues of the Internet in such a smarmy way my books & I will be stigmatized forever after.

I shrink at the prospect. I have carved out a comfort zone here. Even if Mom & Dad could have afforded to send me to Rhodes or Cape Town I think I'd have rather stayed here & gotten on with it myself. Now I am established, I'm something of a stock figure, no one questions my methods, my results speak for themselves, the Head keeps his weary distance from my turf. I am not particularly personable with the boys but I know they respect me. I like to think over the years they have even appreciated the rigours I put them through, beating into them the rectitude of academic integrity. They'd never say so of course & I don't really mind that. My harshness & hostility become me with something of a legacy I'd hate to tarnish, even now as the last days draw near.

So Edwards was biding his time & I wasn't really up for it. When he finally reacted I was almost half fearful of the challenge. We exchanged blows for a good five minutes with me barely holding my own before I was saved by the bell. I haven't felt as loose-footed in the classroom for many a year. I think Edwards sensed I was off colour as well. As he left he gave me one of those wilful smiles of his, brimming with adolescent triumph, yet hesitant too, almost a glimmer of concern if I read him correctly.

'Don't worry – I'll have a comeback for you next lesson,' I said, joking to reassure him.

'I'll look forward to it, sir,' he said & was gone.

What is to become of me? Above everything I fear death at the chalkboard, pinned up & left hanging there in a final moment of humiliation when one day I just won't have the answer, the next step in the argument. I'll stutter & stammer & thumb nervously at the pages of a text book I never use. All will be so utterly undone.

21 October

Every day when I drive in from school I tell myself the electricity's come back & every day I'm disappointed. Accompanied by a sudden rage that only lasts a moment. My general mood plummets thereafter. Can't seem to stop it though I feel it coming on.

I got home today & found myself quite supine only moments later, sprawled on the bed, fighting back the waves of sleep that flowed in a wash of tedium, moroseness, lethargy. I lapsed into a deep sleep & woke much later with the dark around me. Tobias had locked everything up & gone off for the night. I fumbled for the candle he always leaves by my bed when this happens – I suppose he stoops in while I'm dead to the world, snoring my lazy, indolent head off. Truth is I'm lost in some distantly breaking desperation that I am somehow managing to keep just at bay. It's as if I know it's there somewhere, just beyond the fringes, a bend in a path, or a wall of some description, beyond which is an allusive entanglement, something in the grey mists. Only I know at this stage not to ford it, to hold back. The school term still has four weeks left so I know not to go there. I've got to tell myself to maintain my rigid demeanour in front of the boys. Don't go cracking at the edges.

Maybe just a bad day. Maybe I exaggerate.

23 October

V. tired. Still no news from Veronica re. the house. No update from any of the neighbours re. the power outage. Really must sort out meat situation tomorrow! No news of the ongoing political agreement saga. Haven't picked up a paper in days. School weary. The return 'match' with Edwards never materialized in the upper six today. I set them an essay question from a past paper & then watched them moodily get on with it. Felt like a cop-out. Felt like a fucking coward.

24 October

School taxing – these long, tedious Thursdays. The double lower six, followed by the double upper six. Got v. hot by lunch so everyone was in a steamy, foul mood. By 8th period the boys were playing up, hot & bothered themselves. Wanting to talk about sport & girls & parties, etc. instead of work. They ought to know better with me, but sometimes too I tend to forget they're only youngsters. Really, the term can't end soon enough. For those of us who are leaving, this is especially true. Lots to tie up before then – year-ends to mark & grade, reports to write. How does one say encouraging things about the next term when one is deserting the sinking ship? The crew is jumping, the passengers are left on board. 'This was a pleasing examination result for Johnny. I wish him all the best for next year's finals.' Somehow seems patronizing. Seems as if a trust is being broken, a bond forfeited. Feeling low about it.

I overheard snatches of a conversation in the staffroom: someone thought they saw Alicia Wall in the distance at the shops. So is it true? Could it be so? I admit I sit here & am aquiver with thoughts of the tantalizing possibilities. Images of her throng my head, desire runs strong in my blood to have her one more time, to sate myself with lust. But I remember our chequered past. The awkwardness of our prior break-up. Then it hits me, as if it were a completely new realization: I'm to be gone from this place in a mere two & a half months. What room is there for courting in an agenda of upheaval & chaos?

25 October

New domestic woe on the horizon I fear. I got home & Tobias put a pot on the gas cooker & brought me tea. I noticed that he hovered for a moment before withdrawing back to the kitchen. I knew right away something was up. I can understand their edginess: I must have it out with them about the future, what happens when I'm gone, etc.

Only it wasn't that. He was mincing garlic – the God-awful smell permeated the whole house & determined not to fall into my usual afternoon stupor I went outdoors & walked about the garden for a bit. It's been raining more often than not lately but the sun was out, piercing the thick swabs of clouds. The late afternoon light drenching the lawns, glistening at angles off the shrubs, etc. Once I'd rounded the house I saw Tobias standing outside the kitchen door & noticed the poise of his stance.

'Excuse me, baas,' he began.

I sensed this was coming. He rolled up his left trouser leg & showed me a small sore on his shin, just above his ankle. Didn't look terribly serious. My initial reaction was to fob him off. It looked to me like a mosquito bite, albeit a bit inflamed, with a distinct puckered dot at its centre. Slight swelling. But he told me he's had it now for over a week & in the last few days his whole leg has begun to ache.

'Ah, very sore,' he exclaimed, 'very very sore, baas.'

I didn't take this remark at all seriously. I know he's a good old munt in that sort of way, but I do know he's given to exaggeration. (I remember the whole 'Big, big nyoka, baas, big, big!' fuss when I was a boy which turned out to be a tiny brown house snake coiled in the garage.) Endearing in a way & harmless, but slightly devious in others. (The day he came running to report that Sixpence had been on an all-night binge again after pay day, though he hadn't really.)

So I gave him two Disprin from the bottle in the pantry. It never ceases to surprise me how it always does the trick with any of their ailments. They're none the wiser. Could be the placebo effect. Let's see.

26 October
Nothing to report. Dug out my old portable radio & thumbed about trying to pick up the BBC World Service. No luck really,

not helped by batteries which soon ran down. Rumours abounded in the staffroom at lunch about a whole truckload of opposition activists being rounded up in the night & marched off to the cells. Unnerving development. The wavering, tottering unity government can hardly stay together under normal circumstances, let alone when pushed to the brink by such a blatant provocation. It's all such a scam. Who do they think they're kidding? It's more clear now than ever that they never intended to enter into the spirit of power sharing, of reconciliation. The opposition were mad to do a deal, sign up for this abuse, water down their principles by hopping into bed with the enemy. Everyone seems to forget – I think they forget too – that they won the fucking election. One is tempted to grab them by the scruff of the neck & yell, 'Get off your timid bloody arses & fight for your rights. The people spoke loud & clear!' But I guess they had little choice when virtually every neighbouring head of state chooses to turn a blind eye. Anyway, all I write is irrelevant as the preserve of politics in this place takes no account of the will of the people, esp. a young white male. I ought to be furious that beyond the pages of this journal I don't have a voice, but I'm not really. There's an indifference that sits over me like a cloud all of a sudden. I used to care, I used to be passionate about the outcome of events in which I – as a citizen of this country by birth – thought I could help determine. But there is no easier killer of an optimist than the cold cruel workings of an African 'democracy'.

27 October

Yesterday – increasingly desperate over the state of the freezers – I siphoned ten litres of petrol from one of the jerrycans into a small container. Just before cricket practice I stopped off at the area depot for the electricity authority. Went through all the formalities: waited in line, made my official report, got the standard lowdown: fault in the area, no fuel for their vehicles, shortage of technicians, etc. I anticipated all of this. So when I offered my ten litres to fuel their truck (I know, I know), I expected they would accept the offer, thinking I'd gain some leverage to try to pin the operations manager down to a specific pledge to fix the fault at the earliest opportunity, etc. All went according to plan & I went away under the impression that by lunchtime, the power would be restored.

And when I get home today . . .?

I flew into an unimaginable rage. Slammed the car door shut, strode to the house, chucked the clutch of house keys at the bread bin & swore at the top of my voice: 'Fucking arseholes!' Added to this, as if on cue, I could smell that all too familiar fetid odour starting to drift from the freezer. I'd been meaning to pack the meat into cooler boxes & take it round to Ron & Linda, but thought I'd get away with it one day longer. I stormed down the passage & sat on the bed. I could feel my heart thudding in my chest, my breathing was sharp, laboured. I thought to myself: it's days like these when I know exactly why I'm getting out of this dump.

Everything is quiet & still & mournful without the power. No thrum of energy about the house, about me. Everything lifeless. Ironically exactly the opposite of what I felt a few days ago. It's no longer romantic. Just then Tobias hobbled into the bedroom carrying tea on a tray. My initial reaction was to think he was overplaying his limp, I'm sure to goad my attention & sympathy. I must've looked at him coldly because he stopped dead in his tracks, unsure what to do next.

'Just put it there and get out,' I hissed.

I fell into my mattress, cussing & cursing the world. I lay there on my side staring at the walls. Soon I felt numbness come over me & swiftly my eyes were pulled towards deep nothingness.

Now I'm wide awake & it's late & I'm feeling rather ashamed. It's raining: in the stillness I can hear the water drum on the roof.

29 October

Tobias has been wary of me for a few days. My attitude: so be it. I haven't paid too much attention to him, whether he's limping or not. The power's still out & to rub salt into the wound, that ten litres I wasted could've run the generator for close on eight hours. Have chucked all the meat from the upright – ominous watery pools of blood started to appear, leaking from the trays. When we opened it up the smell was putrid. 'Just throw everything away,' I instructed Tobias. I've decided the loss in monetary terms is not worth the loss of sleep I'll have if I actually worked it out. No word from Veronica – must remember to give her a call. Nothing new breaking on the political front. Apparently the activists are still imprisoned. Rumours rife of torture in the cells. Totally outrageous! Am reminded of Plutarch: 'Draco's laws were written not with ink but blood.'

Lots of rain today. Tinkled the ivories a bit: tried to pick out snatches of Chopin, Liszt, Debussy on the piano in the dark but didn't get v. far.

30 October

Finally got round to Ron & Linda's to store what's left of the meat in their big freezer. The first thing Linda said to me was, 'Ian, you've lost weight.'

'Have I?' I replied. 'I hadn't noticed.'

Should I be flattered or concerned?

As warm as ever they invited me to stay for supper, insisting when I tried to back out. I'm glad I did. Linda produced the most amazing spread – roast fillet, Yorkshire pudding & veggies. How the other half live. I sat there, tucking in & realized just how much I've been missing out on over the past few days. It doesn't occur to me to feel deprived when I'm on my own at home, but in comparison to the splendour of the Wilsons', with their grand mansion in the hills & all the electricity you can shake a stick at (for now), I did begin to feel a little resentful. A hot meal in a man's stomach, a few lights to brighten the night-time, a good soak in a hot tub – not much to ask for, is it? Life's little luxuries. Suppose it's a grand deal more than the poor so-called liberated sod gets living in the shanties & squatter camps.

'Touch wood, the power's not so bad here,' Ron said. 'I think there must be a fat cat living up the road, so we're more or less taken care of by default.'

Lucky you, I felt like saying, living in an area where every other NGO executive & gvt minister has a luxury pad.

'So is it true,' Linda said, 'you are definitely off then?'

'I'm afraid so.'

'No turning back this time?'

'No. The house is on the market. I've resigned. I've applied for a new job. It looks as if it's a done deal. Hanging on any longer just doesn't seem an option anymore.'

'Such a pity. I'm sure the school is kicking themselves.'

I shrugged. 'Don't know really. They'll replace me I'm sure.'

Ron said, 'Can't be easy, after sticking it out all these years. But don't think South Africa's the golden ticket. Their problems are only just beginning.'

'Surely you've thought of Australia?' Linda asked.

'I have. But it's the passport issue & the immigration process is just killing.'

'Come on – someone as educated as yourself?'

'Well, they're not really in need of academics I don't think. Hairdressers & refrigeration technicians yes. And I'd never want to teach there – I've heard the kids have no respect for authority. Besides, I don't really feel I can leave Africa entirely. I don't know, it's sort of my domain.'

'Your poor mother, I'm sure she'd have loved to have one of her sons close by.'

This carried on for some time in a similar vein. All v. nice & tidy. Then Ron said, 'News is they're trying to get rid of all us NGOs. So the honeymoon is finally over. Apparently we're seen as spies of the West now, sympathizers of the opposition.'

'Christ, it's like the bloody Cold War,' I said.

'I don't know, truth be told, if we'll manage to hold out much longer here ourselves the way they're carrying on. Everyone & everything is an enemy threat to them. Their own paranoia is what's driving them now. We're the single largest aid donor in sub-Saharan Africa & what thanks do we get? I'm convinced I've got the CIO tailing me day & night, our trucks get stopped, searched, regularly looted & diverted exclusively to the loyalists they're desperate to keep happy. It's all about food control now. Who has it & who can give to who. And all they rant about is how Britain has imposed illegal sanctions against their nation! How can you call sixty million pounds a year in aid "illegal sanctions"?'

'It's tunnel vision, Ron,' I said. 'The only reason they call it sanctions is because they perceive targeted travel bans & asset freezes that only apply to a handful of them as being the end of the world. They assume by extension they apply to every citizen because they care about no one but themselves. Plus, it's all just an excuse to try & get the European banks to unlock their accounts.'

'It's the height of selfishness,' Linda added. 'They have no idea what charities & aid organizations do for this country, how they prop it up, keep it going.'

'Indirectly,' I said. 'I mean no offence, Ron, but it's such organizations that prolong the misery in the long run, that keep giving the dying beast a further breath.'

'True, but it's catch-22, Ian. What are we supposed to do? Sit back while three-quarters of the population starve to death because a bunch of thugs has decided to prolong its glorified plunder of the country's resources?'

'Yes, yes, quite right,' I said. The conversation was getting a little heated. In the end I couldn't help but sympathize with poor Ron. Despite the protected executive lifestyle, despite having a passport at his disposal that gets him back to Britain in a flash, it's still tough when you're being pushed out of something by forces beyond your control.

In all the years I've known Ron & Linda, going back to the days when Ron was Dad's regular fly-fishing pal up in the Highlands & we all used to have family trips together to the National Parks cottages by Mare Dam, I don't think I've ever seen them as despondent as tonight. What is wrong with everybody?

1 November
Went to school, taught badly, came home. Exam revision – boring as hell & I think the boys can sense my indifference.

Tobias cooked up something for me on the gas plate for dinner. Spaghetti with tomato & bacon sauce. Hope the bacon hasn't gone off. Stopped off on the way home & bought four big ice blocks. Crazily had to go to three different garages at three different shopping centres: the first two had power cuts! For a bag of water shoved in a freezer overnight they certainly charge a premium – been muttering all evening about it. Still, it keeps the big freezer going for a bit.

Tried to reread bits of *Antigone*. Why, I don't know. Lessons in tyranny, etc. Ancient & modern: man has never been more the same! Anyway, candlelight too weak. Can barely see what I'm scrawling here. Will go off & wash in the water Tobias leaves in the bucket that's so cold it shocks the flesh like a zap & soaks down to the bones.

2 November

Phoned Veronica during a free at school. 'Oh, my darling,' she said, 'I was just about to call you.' Good appeasement strategy. 'Great news – I have an interested viewer. Would tomorrow afternoon suit?'

'I suppose,' I said.

'Two thirty?'

'Fine. But I must warn you – the power's been off for days. Things aren't as pristine as they could be.'

'But, darling,' she retorted, 'what's new?'

Have been living in dread ever since.

3 November

As expected, the day was a trying one. Arrived back home at 1.30 already in a state of some anxiousness. Can't exactly say now what I felt, or explain why I felt it. Almost the knowledge that I'm wedged in a paradox of sorts: the defensive instinct of being wary of strangers in one's home & yet the simultaneous need to make them feel they can possess it. I walked around certain rooms thinking I'd rather they didn't see this photo, or this painting, or snoop around my bedroom or peer at the toilet seat. Tobias & I went to some lengths to spruce the place up, clearing away the clutter. (As it turns out such considerations appear redundant: they only seem interested in the physical construction of the house these days, not its ambiance, its homeliness, so Veronica tells me. 'They'll probably just rip it all out anyway, darling, and start over.')

I guess what really upsets me – apart from my space being invaded – is that I still don't have a really clear, absolute reason for deciding to sell. Just as in the same way, I couldn't confess to this journal – or perhaps 'express' is a better word – in *real* terms a reason for the day I walked into Muller's office & handed in my notice. I cited practical reasons only: economics, remuneration, the prospect of all-out anarchy. He sat there looking shell-shocked. Poor sod. I was the fourth member of staff so far this term. Maybe he thought we were calling his bluff: he knew that we didn't really know the real reasons. He knows that we've survived so far on the salaries we get, & have put up with the decline for so many years that we could probably carry on doing so indefinitely. The lot of the stoic. We'll always make a plan to overcome the odds: that's what's defined us Zimbabweans for so long. It's what makes us a breed on our own.

Along came Veronica, all kisses & hugs, the usual fawning fatuousness. Stuffed into a short, tight, denim skirt. After her a Mercedes came in. A bald Greek businessman. Pale grey suit & dark shades. Looked very severe, critical, stony. Sweaty face. Veronica fell all over him but he wasn't moved. He made a cursory inspection, grumbling & groaning in heavy Greek. At the end of it he stood in the driveway shrugging his shoulders, his palms upturned, weighing his opinions from hand to hand.

'Sure, it's an okay place,' he announced. 'But I have to ask this –
does Tasso want to buy property at this time in such a country?
Such a basket case? Possibly Tasso does want to take a risk. Does
Tasso want to pay top dollar for such a place in such a country?
Hmm . . . Tasso is unsure.'

So he was off, Veronica shrugging, saying, 'You can't please all
of them, darling, but don't worry, something will come up soon.'

It still seems somehow unreal. Kept thinking I was standing in
a scene from a Greek version of *The Godfather*. So I haven't been
too dispirited about the whole encounter as yet. I haven't felt as if
my world is being ripped from under my feet.

4 November

V. hot all day. Cricket practice almost unbearable so took boys for
swim instead. This evening Edwards came round. He'd asked me
some while back if he could go over a few of the common questions
on Paper 2. Not that he needs it. He came racing up the drive in his
little blue Starlet, all done up with flashy rims etc, & the most God-
awful music blaring from what must be the most massive speakers.
We sat out on the veranda. It was only 5.15 & plenty of sunlight left.
I put out some crisps in a bowl & opened two warmish beers & then
tried to remember the last time I'd actually entertained anyone.
Must be the better part of the year. V. shameful.

We went over a question on the Napoleonic wars, one on
Nuremberg & one on the decolonization of Africa. We talked a
great deal, much of it getting v. philosophical & beyond the brief
of the syllabus or the reasons he had come. I recall saying something like, 'History, Nicholas, is simply a matter of strength. Its
only function is to detail the collective power of muscle. The
strong dominate the weak. The powerful conquer the powerless

& then exploit them for their own gains. Colonization is the history of the world in one form or another. What the propaganda machine that runs this place now conveniently forgets is that dozens of African tribes were doing exactly the same thing for centuries before the dreaded Cecil J. Rhodes showed up.'

One day I really ought to finally put pen to paper, fulfil that early promise. Flesh out some polemic on this blighted land & stir a thousand hateful voices in my ears. Anyway, I found it v. stimulating. A fine evening of conversation. Feel much better for it. Before we knew it the light had fallen & we had another warm beer & by candlelight he was regaling me with the current woes of his love life. Juggling two girls at once, it seems. I'm hardly surprised. I'd imagine he's quite a charmer, young Nick Edwards, he has that smoothness of talk & manner. Then he realized it was getting on & went home.

Now all quiet, still, dark.

5 November

Have been missing music on the stereo in the house. When I got home today I had Vaughn Williams' 'The Lark Ascending' on the player in the car & I just killed the engine & pressed back my seat & slumped there, listening to it. I dozed off under a weary, ethereal fog. The solo violin climbing, soaring to the top of my mind, the emptiness. I woke to Sixpence tapping on the window. The sun was setting. I stumbled groggily into the house.

6 November
Morning

I woke in the dark this morning when I heard the rain drumming on the roof. Fumbled for the candle & struck a match. The room wavered greyly in dim snatches of light. Hadn't sleep well. I was still half sunk in a restless stupor when I sloped off to the bathroom. As a madman lost in his own catalepsy of thought, I stripped bare & soaked the sponge with soap & lathered the bitter coldness in the bucket to my body. Wrapped the towel round my waist & lay in the dark again, thinking through those still hours till dawn. I was recalling tracts from *Paradise Lost*. I don't know why. 'And in the lowest deep a lower deep still threatening to devour me opens wide.' The mugginess seemed to linger long after the dark had dispersed.

Evening

Drama of a sort. At six o'clock this morning Tobias was nowhere to be seen with my breakfast tea. His lateness annoyed me but I shaved with the cold water left in the basin & got dressed & left for school. In the fourth I felt a hollow grumbling in my stomach. I was drumming into the dreary lower six the need to reference their essays properly when I felt light-headed but it quickly passed. By break I was starving.

Later, at home, I noticed at once that the house hadn't been cleaned. In the bedroom, the bedding was all rumpled & creased from last night. I walked down to the bottom of the garden to the servants' quarters in something of a temper. The ground was all squelchy & muddy & the rain had pooled into small rivulets beneath my feet. Sixpence was sitting under a yellow plastic tarp knitted together with old fertilizer bags, tied like a sail between the branches of the lemon tree.

'Where's Tobias?' I asked. He pointed to his room. I banged on the door & called out but there was no response. The rain was falling harder, perhaps I didn't hear him. I was getting drenched. I pushed the door open & it grated over the slate stone floor &

stuck. I kicked it impatiently. The red brick and mortar gloom. The sense of perpetual dankness, made considerably worse by the tall piles of clutter & junk. I've never been in Tobias's room before. In one corner stands an old iron wood stove & I saw instantly how caked it was in a thick muck of coalesced black soot. I was drawn to the line of black singed up the brick wall. The ceiling was speckled with a black & grey mould. Disgust filled me. On a small cot pushed against one side of the room, Tobias lay.

'Why haven't you been at work today?' I demanded. He was shirtless, his wrinkled flabby skin hanging loosely from his bony chest as I suppose it does on an old man.

'Sorry, baas, very very sorry.' He pointed to his leg. 'Very very sore it is.'

I took a step forward & squinted down at his ankle. The bite was still there, but it didn't look any bigger. The muscle around his shin was drawn tight & shining a light coppery brown. I don't know if this is usual or not. As far as I could tell it wasn't swollen. By now the rain was thumping on the loose tin roof & in the corner above his cot I could see it was leaking in & dripping down the wall in a neat silvery stream.

'For God's sake,' I began, 'why don't you look after your room properly, hey? Look at this mess in here! It's filthy. No wonder things bite you and you get infected. It's because of the dirt. Now clean this place up.'

I made my way back to the house, trudging through the streaks of mud, getting utterly drenched. I traipsed through to the bathroom & dried myself & lay down on the bed, tired & irascible. I may have begun to snooze, but a while later I felt a presence next to me & a voice said, 'Baas, your tea.'

Later I felt bad. I watched him from behind & his limp is quite pronounced now. I gave him four Disprin. I scoured the medicine chest & found some antiseptic lotion. I gave him the tablets & squeezed a dollop of the lotion onto his finger & told him to rub it in. He looked at it curiously but was grateful nonetheless. I hope this will be the end of it.

7 November

Started marking exam papers. What a bore. What a way to spend the weekend. News on the grapevine that the opposition has demanded the release of all political detainees or else it will withdraw from the unity gvt. As if on cue, the army has apparently intensified intimidation & fear tactics in the southern strongholds. Rounding up villagers, beating them up, pillaging their food. Seems now that whenever a demand is made on them they step up the brutality. And from a party apparently 'committed to a peaceful, political solution to resolving the political stalemate in the nation'. Added to this, someone was talking of a fresh cholera outbreak this morning. All this while here in relative sanity I plough through largely unpromising history essays.

8 November

Marked all afternoon. Neck stiff, eyes strained. The stress intensified by the arrival of night which puts a sudden stop to progress. Then groping around in those waiting hours, knowing there's so much to do. Later this evening, just before it was totally dark, Tobias brought me my supper of tuna in a white sauce with pasta. When I took the tray back to the kitchen, he was sitting on the back step, clutching his foot in clear anguish.

I called to him but he didn't respond. The pain must have been very pronounced. He just sat, quietly humming a woeful tune. I could see his teeth were gritted.

'Just stay here,' I said. 'I'll go call Sixpence.'

I walked halfway down the garden & yelled. Sixpence came running.

'Come,' I said, 'we need to get Tobias to his room.'

Tobias muttered something to Sixpence, shaking his head.

'What's the problem?' I asked.

Sixpence said, 'Baas, he says he needs to go to clinic.'

I must've shaken my head unconsciously or shown some impatience because Tobias looked up & started pleading with me.

'Please, baas,' he said several times, 'it very sore now. Very sore.'

I sighed & thought about it, but I was not at my most sympathetic. I was tired from marking. The thought of getting into the car & going on a trek round town for the sake of an aching leg wasn't one I welcomed.

'No,' I said, 'we can't go now. It's too late. All the clinics will be shut. I'll give you some more tablets. Sixpence can help you get back to your room. We'll go to the clinic tomorrow if it's still sore.'

He half nodded, though I could tell that he was disappointed. Rather than feel any more sorry for him, I became annoyed. I walked inside & shut the kitchen door behind me, leaving the pair of them in the dark.

9 November
Lunchtime

Have received an invitation to a 'drinks reception' at the O'Connors' on Friday evening. A few of the staff have them, hand delivered to our pigeonholes. On very elegant white card, it says, 'Tony & Michelle O'Connor cordially invite you to a drinks reception at 7.00 p.m. at our residence, no. 15 Beaton Close, Greystone Park, on Friday the 11th November, to show our appreciation for your efforts in teaching Michael in his final year.'

Funny how it's always the dimmest prospects who end up being the most gracious. I may well attend.

Otherwise I have finished all scripts. Entered marks on the database & began reports. I can see light at the end of the tunnel. Today I got an e-mail from St James' College confirming my appointment as head of their history department for the start of next year. Details of my package were outlined. A flat in the school grounds, adjacent to the boys' hostel. Basic furnishings included. Meals at communal dining room at a nominal cost, if desired. Medical benefits. 35 per cent pension contributions. The salary nothing exceptional, but certainly a marked improvement. Seems things are falling into place. On the back of this I posted an advert on the web server: 'Household goods for sale. Good quality, tasteful. Cash offers welcome.'

Later

On my way home I stopped off at the electricity depot & tried to pin down the operations manager. Apparently, or so they told me, he'd been called away to fix a fault in a minister's neighbourhood.

'I wish I bloody lived next door to a minister!' I quipped but the remark raised no response. So I asked about the fault they'd promised to fix when I donated ten litres of fuel. The man – some clerk or another – grinned & shook his head. 'Ah, sir, we have big problems here. We are short of spare parts. For that fault we need cable joiners & kits & we don't have any in stock. Also, our vehicle is off the road & needs a new ignition system.'

He took me round the back of a small prefabricated workshop. There were four trucks stationed in a line. Two had their bonnets up, awaiting attention. Another was supported by bricks & had no wheels. There were some seven or eight men in blue overalls – supposedly technicians – all lazing about. Two were playing checkers with bottle tops. A few were dozing in the sun.

'You see the problem, sir?'

'Look, is this fault ever going to get fixed?' I asked.

He looked at me for a while. 'Well if every resident contributes ten US dollars towards spare parts then we can fix it, no problem.'

'And how many residents are in the affected area – how big is the fault?'

'That one – about 100 residents sir.'

'So basically you want 1000 dollars?'

'Yes, sir. You bring direct to me & we'll arrange it to be fixed within the hour.'

'To you directly & you guarantee you can get the part & fix the fault in an hour?'

'Yes, sir, one hour.'

10 November

Where to begin? I was dead tired last night & fell asleep in half an hour, though it was only seven o'clock. I slept well & when I woke it was brighter than usual. The clouds had cleared, the sun was up. Knew at once I'd overslept. No Tobias. I got up & hastily dressed & left the house. By the garage Sixpence came running up to me. Already late for my first lesson, I wasn't in the mood to dally. He wanted to know whether he should go & bring Tobias out so that I could take him to the clinic. I had to breathe in deeply to stop myself from yelling.

'Can't you see he's already made me late? I don't have time now.' He stood there stone-faced. 'Okay, look, here's what you can do – you go with him this morning to the small general clinic on Second Street. It's only three kilometres away & it's free. Take him there & get him sorted out proper, see?'

I handed him ten dollars. 'If it isn't free this should be enough. If it is, bring the money back.'

When I reversed out he was still standing there clutching the note. When I got home from school at lunch he was weeding the grass by the back door. 'Well? All sorted?' I asked him. He stood up shaking his head.

'No, baas. There is no one there. Whole place empty & shut.'

This came as little surprise. I didn't react. But I knew I couldn't put it off any longer. I told him to help bring Tobias to the car.

'We'll try a different clinic,' I said.

It took an age for him to hobble – propped up by Sixpence – from his quarters to the garage. I could see now that he was in some pain. He could barely manage to put an inkling of pressure on that foot & whenever he did, his face convulsed into a tight ball of anguish. Eventually we got him to the car & he shuffled in.

Drove to the semi-pvt clinic in Glen Lorne. I'd thought they'd gone bust but when I was relating the whole saga to Janet over break, she mentioned she'd recently taken her maid there & that she'd found them 'good enough'. About a ten-minute drive away, over the hills & past the school & into the affluence of Glen Lorne. Lots of expansive, ostentatious mansions of the nouveau riche have popped up since I was last in the area. Towering colossal above lines of fir trees, acres of rolling, manicured grass, etc. V. distasteful.

Found the clinic easily enough. Only a few cars in the car park but a long line of people snaked towards the entrance. An ominous sign. Already I could feel my temper flinching (a psychosomatic reaction to the mere sight of a queue?). I parked & told Tobias to wait & walked to the entrance. V. shabby inside. Weak-green, plastic-coated tiled floor, peeling in large chunks. Grubby plastic chairs which were all taken. A few people squatting on the floor. A nice little pastiche of chaos. A muddle of the sick & ailing. The screams of a snotty-nosed baby. The wail of a delirious woman lying half unconscious on the floor. It stank of stale perspiration & sickness. A nurse was giving orders from behind a counter in a raised voice, trying to keep control. I waited, already ruing the decision to come at all.

She proved difficult. Party loyalist I suspect. She found the circumstances – of an employer bringing his worker for treatment – to be most irregular.

'No, no, no, he must come & register himself,' she said. 'If he is not a juvenile he can come on his own.'

I explained to her why he was waiting in the car but she was even less impressed.

'No, no, he must come. I need to see all patients in person.'

I gave her a bemused stare & started walking back to the car. The queue had lengthened. I turned & went back in.

'Look,' I said, 'how long will it take to see the doctor?'

'The queue is there,' she said, 'you can see yourself.'

'Right, so if I bring him in & he registers & then I pay a little extra, would he be able to see the doctor a little quicker?'

She looked at me sternly. 'What are you saying? Do you think you are special? There is a queue. Can you not see the queue? That is where every patient must wait their turn. Is it because the colour of your skin is different to mine that—'

There was nothing for it. You just can't corrupt some people. I went outside to the car & fetched Tobias. He was limping but he could walk. We went back to the desk & he registered. Took an age. Not an easy task for a man who has never had a formal education. The nurse seemed belligerent every time I tried to help him. I paid the nominal ten-dollar fee & we went outside.

'Just join this line here, okay & wait to see the doctor,' I said. 'You'll be okay to wait here?'

He nodded & didn't protest & went limping off to join the queue which was some thirty people long. I sat in the car & tracked down my CD of Chopin's *Nocturnes* & let it pipe about me. Nothing like a little genius to sate the wounded soul.

I was listless for a while, despite the music, & I became tired quickly, saturated with boredom. I slipped my seat back & soon found myself slumped against the window, my head tossed back for a while, then rolling about my shoulder. I was drifting off, curiously sedated by the warmth of the car's interior, the light fragrant smell of the lavender spray Sixpence uses to polish the dashboard, the vanilla cream he uses to shine the leather seats. I wasn't unhappy there, my mind free to drift, my body absent from school & the quiet restiveness of the unpowered house where the tensions of life lie exposed, those open wounds. With the CD playing I was hardly aware of the figure standing beside my window, tapping at me.

The light had dulled. I opened the back door & Tobias prized his way in. He was panting hard. His jaw clenched, his cheeks drawn in, his eyes burning hard. One hand clutched his ankle. In the other he held something.

'What did they say?' I asked. He opened his palm to reveal a small plastic packet of tablets. I looked at the label: Paracetamol.

'Is this all they gave you?' He nodded. He turned his head from me, hiding some inner fury or maybe a gleam of emotional strain. Strange to suddenly have that intimacy exposed between us after all these years of being committed to the distant aloofness of our master/servant trope. I leant over & patted his knee.

'They didn't say anything else?'

He shook his head.

'Don't worry,' I said. I tried to sound reassuring. 'These tablets are good. Better than the ones at home, hey. Much stronger.'

He said nothing, nor did he turn to look at me. I was tired now & started the car & reversed out, past the patients reeling off from the queue. I didn't make any conscious observations of them at the time, although now, when I think over it, when I sit here in the dark & confess to my own insensitivities, I can swear they were all looking down at the packets of painkillers in their hands. Each & every one of them treated the same. Cattle in the kraal, getting vaccinated, getting shunted through the run.

Past midnight

Can't sleep a wink. Keep tossing & turning. Some close dread in the outer dark. Got up & fumbled for the candle & stalked down the passage to my desk. Everything in these lone hours seems invested with some pretence, some rejection of my presence. It's as if the air objects to my woken conscience stealing from it that which I'm only entitled to by day. Strange observation. Shakespeare's *Twelfth Night* – 'There is no darkness but ignorance.' Maybe that's it. Maybe I'm just ignorant. Maybe the absence of light in my life – not just the physical light of bulbs & lamps – but a light, *the* light, light itself, is the manifestation of my tantamount ignorance to all that surrounds me. The degree certificates framed

& hung on the wall beside this desk where I write exonerate me from nothing, nothing at all. How stupid to assume they lift me above anything. I really ought to haul myself back to bed.

11 November

Have finished reports, tied up all loose ends re. admin. Now it's just a waiting game. Tap, tap, my fingers on the desk. I floated the idea of trying to text to Alicia's old number, test the waters, try my luck. Something was holding me back – perhaps fear of rejection, or even worse, silence.

Since the trip to the clinic I haven't heard much about Tobias's ailment. To be honest I'm reluctant to ask. Trying to avoid engaging him in too much conversation. We seem to stay out of one another's way as if by some unspoken agreement. He's still hobbling about badly but seems more resigned to it than before. I go about my routine & he goes about his chores & I'm beginning to think that I've heard the last on the matter. I hope this is the case: strangely, the whole affair's been playing on my conscience.

12 November
Saturday mid-morning.

Slept well after a rather heady evening. The notion of a sedate 'drinks reception' at the O'Connors' turned out to be a lavish bash, with no expense spared on catering (the most scrumptious spread imaginable), a full bar, a disco & a whole cross-section of guests ranging from other parents, O'Connor's mates (almost the entire upper six), a whole bevy of young girls clutching onto them & several fellow staff. The house is a huge sprawling affair perched on the side of a hill with substantial rolling gardens. All lit up with angled spots. Long, classical-style pool & a wide terrace too where everyone was congregated. The accompanying girlfriends all Lolita-like in vulgar miniskirts & tops that barely covered their midriffs. God knows what was going on behind the bushes.

Felt decidedly cringing at first, but soon mingled in with the staff & parents, all of whom I have come to know pretty well over the six years their sons have been at the school. More than one set came up to me & said how sorry they were that I was leaving after so many years & 'such a reputation' as that horsey Joan Henson said. Vicky Edwards said, 'Nicholas has just loved all the discussions you've had together.' Felt v. flattered, then a bit flat. Suddenly that first twinge of realizing I'm actually going started to flare up. Nonetheless I braced myself & continued to mingle. Muller & his Mrs were there, grim-faced as ever. Then that coquette Stacey Brisk latched onto me, glass of wine in hand & seemed determined not to let go. It seems she thinks our friends with benefits arrangement still stands, though it's been over a year since I ventured down that dark alley. (A whole year?)

A bit later we all started to mingle more. We all had far too much to drink. The boys were all v. hospitable & cheered us staff on, etc. This was after the Mullers had gone & even before we all played immature drinking games with shooters of neat lemon-scented vodka. Vile. Then a group of them disappeared into the house & up the stairs to a room, insisting I go with them. We went out through open French doors to a balcony. The lights of the city spattered rather thinly below us. Somewhere in that dark splurge was this neighbourhood, this house which hasn't seen a touch of electricity for three weeks. O'Connor, Ncube & Henson were fiddling on a wrought-iron table with a packet of something. I stood looking out, talking to a quite inebriated Edwards.

'Fuck am I glad school's over sir,' he said.

'What are your plans, Nick?' I asked.

He steadied up & said, 'Don't know, just get out.'

'Out where?'

He shrugged & gestured with his arms at the air. 'This fucking shithole, what else?' I knew at once he meant not only the city, the country, but the placeless redundancy, the toxic sterility, the contagious sensibilities of being a white boy in Africa. At once I saw in him the courage I'd never had when I was eighteen, bookish & antisocial, withdrawing into a shell & mistakenly thinking I had a place here, a future, instead of getting out into the real world where the history attached to the colour of my skin wasn't going to end up being a liability, a target, a weight of debt.

'Good,' I said. 'That's what someone like you needs, Edwards.'

'And you too, sir,' he added. He was looking at me quite intently across that limp sodium light & our eyes met in a moment of stern intensity as if things had been reversed now & he was instructing me & I needed to take heed of his advice. I don't think he was referring to just South Africa either. I nodded.

Just then the others came round all clutching spliffs they'd been busy rolling. They handed me one. I was hesitant to take it at first, but they all said, 'Come on, Mr H, live a little.'

Then Ncube said, 'We just want to say, sir, thanks for everything.'

I was completely taken aback.

'You weren't the easiest dude to have as a teacher but we'll never forget your lessons, sir. We sure learned a thing or two about life. Thanks from all of us & good luck in your new job.'

With that we all took a deep drag on the spliff. I didn't know what to say. I just smiled at them & nodded appreciatively. I'm

119

sure they could see I was fighting back the gleam welling in my eyes. I knew it was time to leave.

I'm sitting here now plunging my mind for parallels with the classics, something ageless & vindicating I can quote from the sages on the innocence of hedonism or the justification of excess. What I really ought to be doing is acknowledging the unbridled comradeship of man.

13 November

Two trying developments re. the house. Veronica phoned early to say she had another viewer. We set up an appointment at three o'clock. A Chinese man this time, short & stocky & dressed in a severe blue suit. My heart sank. My contempt rooted purely in the belief that they're only piling in here by the plane load to mop up everything we leave behind. (And the gvt rants & raves about the threat of recolonization!)

'I look to make Chinese lestalant,' he announced.

'Of course you do, darling,' Veronica replied, patting him on the shoulder. 'Now come this way, Mr Lin.'

He stood looking at the driveway. 'Must have big livelay for car park. Fifty car they must fit.'

Then in the kitchen: 'No, no, this kitchen too small.' He shook his head vigorously. 'We go now please.'

Later I phoned Veronica & told her bluntly: no more Greeks or Chinese.

'The market's dead as a doornail,' she tells me. 'No one wants to invest.'

'Just keep trying,' I said.

Then at about 4.30 I got a call from a woman looking to buy household goods. When she arrived at 5 p.m. she handed me a business card – 'Express Auctions'. Not what I wanted to see. She nosed about, prodding & poking at all & sundry. Looked as if she had a bad smell under her nose the whole time but I persevered with her. Made a few notes & said she'd give me a call.

Now I'm feeling very disconcerted about the whole encounter. I keep getting this flash-forward to some dingy, dusty, overcrowded warehouse where all the world & his dog gather to scrutinize & bid on the contents of your life. 'Lot no. 28, one queen-size bed, pine, with ornamental woodwork & side drawers, lockable. Posturepedic mattress. Slept in by thirty-one-year-old male, tall, educated, white. Only rare occasions of coitus. Not particularly adventurous sexually. No pets to compensate for lack of company.'

14 November

Tobias has been busy. When I got home I immediately sniffed mukwa oil & saw a light drying film of it across the parquet tiles. The smell always kindles an unplaced satisfaction: fuel & linseed & something organic altogether. Everything's been dusted & polished. A glint to every surface.

Then his motives were revealed. He was hovering again, just out the corner of my eye the whole time. I decided to broach the issue directly.

'How's your leg?' I asked him.

He turned from the sink & said, 'Ah, baas, it is still very bad.'

'And those tablets they gave you at the clinic – they haven't worked?'

He shook his head. 'They not work that well, baas. It still very sore all the time.'

We stood looking at each other for some moments. I didn't really have anything more I could say or offer on the matter.

Then he said, 'Baas, I think I go back to my homelands to get better.'

'Homelands – are you mad?'

'No, baas, I go to see traditional healer man.'

'Traditional healers aren't the answer,' I tried to tell him. 'He'll only rub some or another ointment on & rattle some bones & that'll be that.'

'No, baas—'

'Plus, have you not heard that the rural areas are not good places now? There's lots of problems there. The army, the cholera, beatings & looting.'

He looked at me blankly.

'Don't you listen to that radio of yours?'

'The radio say everything going to be good here again. It say all problems are fault of England & America.'

I sighed. I felt truly despairing for him. But nothing I say is going to get through to him. He's not going to be bullied by me.

'When will you come back?' I asked.

He lowered his eyes & didn't answer. I took this to mean: I'm not coming back. What's there to come back to?

'Well go,' I said sharply, 'but when your supply of tablets runs out, you'll be on your own, hey.'

The more I think of it, the more I fret. This strange limbo we're living through. No one knows who's coming or going. There's a troubled dispensation in this country & ever since that disputed election & the shaky power-sharing deal, we've all been paralyzed, a void which resonates uneasily about everyone. Nothing's happening, but everything is. We're always on the verge of outright anarchy, but somehow not quite. Behind the scenes, in the depths of the country, villages that hardly have a name on a map are being levelled to the ground. I'm nervous thinking of Tobias caught up in it all. He's innocent & weak, just an old man wanting to get to a destination. He's been a loyal old soul. To my parents, to me. All these years.

16 November

No sign of power. Have almost given up worrying. In the meantime I've streamlined my life. Something tinned for supper, usually. Tuna, sardines, ham, lots of pasta. I'm ambivalent. In the end I've finally decided to text Alicia. Surprisingly I got a message straight back. Confirms she's back in the country after being abroad, working in London. Suggested we meet. Intriguing, but somehow, despite initiating it, I feel reticent. Still I replied: 'Of course, definitely, can't wait 2 C U,' etc. Probably sounded like some desperately horny teenager. We'll see.

17 November

Well that's that. He's gone. Went off this morning. I hadn't been expecting it to be this sudden. I thought of telling him to stay till the month's end, but what difference does it make? I squared up with him & gave him a fairly handsome gratuity & money for the bus fare, plus a whole lot of old clothes I was throwing out anyway in a tatty brown suitcase. He'd packed all his possessions into his little knapsack. The rest of his belongings, he says, he's organized for his nephew to pick up in a truck. He wore his Sunday church suit & looked dapper in his faded fawn trousers & tan checked jacket & a navy-blue tie. I noticed he was wearing the maroon shirt I gave him in his Christmas box last year & found this v. touching. He also donned a wide-brimmed hat, the kind a cricket umpire might wear, only brown, & held a wooden cane in his free hand which he used as a support for his bad leg. He docked his hat at me & smiled politely & we shared a few memories, a few anecdotes of his recollections of me as an infant, with my mother & father & my brothers. Then he hobbled off down the driveway & out the gate. Slowly down the road he went, walking away from thirty-eight years of service, from a place I'd imagine he called his home. For some reason I want to record this image v. precisely.

'Be careful, old man,' I called after him as he went away down the road. 'Get to your home in one piece, hey!'

He lifted his hat one more time in acknowledgement. I turned from the gate & went indoors.

18 November

Have been depressed all day. It isn't exactly the knowledge that he's not coming back, or that things are going to stack up beyond control, or that the power's been out for well over a month. It's the process that has started to unravel around me, the process of elimination. It's the atmosphere in the house, the atmosphere of rejection. By osmosis, it knows I'm abandoning it & it's gone cold, frigid, indifferent on me. It's the loneliness.

Yes, it's the loneliness & somehow, with Tobias now gone, it seems the last link to my childhood, my youth, my family has vanished for good. I sit here & can honestly say I have no idea when I'll next see Mom & Dad, Alex or James. For they are flung in all directions & I can't see how I'd ever afford to get to them all. I can't see myself arriving in Toronto to see Alex & the Canadian wife I've never met, the woman from a foreign icy place he's coupled with & produced two offspring, a girl with cherry locks & a chubby boy, who'll both grow up in a welfare state & speak with

124

a twang & not have an inkling that pumping through their veins is the sun & heat & dust of Africa. And James, in the crowded misery of London, working in the bland IT field. Screwing loose girls he picks up easily, drunk in overcrowded pubs. He moves amongst people who have no feel for space, for the wide expanses of the plains of the lowveld, the bush where man treads a tenuous step, ever subservient to the calls & beasts of the wild. He tramps the concrete streets & rushes for buses & is pushed along with the masses onto an underground train & in certain solitary moments he has unbidden memories – this I know to be true – of playing French cricket with his brothers on the big back lawn of this his boyhood home, of roasting mealie cobs with Tobias over bricks at the back of the garage, of Mother's chicken casseroles.

3

All the while the provisions are whittling down. When they stop and tip the water container, the meniscus lowers ever more, and the angle at which they have to tilt it becomes more acute. It's almost painful to watch. The lip of the Coke bottle is too narrow and the prospect of losing even a drop of water is so grave that they make a funnel with an empty bean can that they squash and hammer into the shape of a cone. Their path has not taken them to any active river or stream. Coming down off a low knoll one afternoon they drew parallel to a riverbed, a bare grassless basin, the pale loam hard and dry. There where the bones of some beast had fallen into the sand as if its airy shell were still kneeling and burrowing its neck into the trough. The man stood and glassed over the dryness and a visible dejection took hold of him. A boy promised a toy he will never have. He had been expecting to come across water. He had been measuring out their stores bit by bit. They had little left in reserve.

The food must be running low too. Every time they dip a hand into the sacks they bring out less and less. But each time they do something is produced that is more than nothing, more than the empty held-out palm. Their stores seem bottomless, blessed by some proverb or watched over by some atavistic numen. Or else they are simply thrifty in the extreme, pilgrim-like in their consumption and they know well the parable of division: a little broken into many many parts. Sometimes when they aren't so tired the man will remember a word of thanksgiving before the mealie cakes or the mashed dried fish or the thin cobs are eaten. Sometimes he will hold out his upturned palms and raise them to the level of his face and, closing his eyes, mutter something which may be a prayer or an offering to the ancestors. At other times he forgets and they all sit hunched and drawn and melancholic, rolling the food in their fingers, pressing it into small balls in their hands and bringing it forlornly to their mouths. They take nothing for granted.

The boys' free time is set aside for the chore of scouring beyond the threadbare glades for trees they may pick and plunder. Once they came across a tree with crisp white petals, calyces covered in rust-coloured hairs. Its thick pods had fallen flush to the ground. The boys went forth with an empty sack and brought back a whole load to the campsite. They sat about chewing the ripe pods and discarding the others. They slipped the edge of the machete blade between the crevice and cranked them open, splitting them like oyster or mussel shells. There were plenty to go round. They came over and dropped so many before him his eyes could not digest the mound piled at his feet. His mouth filled with juices he had not known for some time. It may have been as good as gnawing at vegetables found unexpectedly in an abandoned patch.

They walk by day, rest mostly by night. They don't come across another living thing for some time. A stretch of days that may seem longer than it really is. The path leads on through this maze in the bush. It winds and forks and they wind and fork with it. The pain in his feet grows intolerable. His back hurts. They slap his backside or spine often with the flat of the machete. Soon the bow of his ribs begins to pout a cage round his chest. He is losing weight, getting weaker. There is a sore at his neck that oozes at night and dries to a sticky scab in the sun. It gets worse.

The woman veers between schizophrenic states like a chameleon. Her babe wedged inside her, clamped in its incubating cell. The lanky boys stoop along and the man too. The machetes and the rifle. The radio that once in a while they huddle round, surfing the airwaves in vain until finally the batteries die altogether and there is only silence. Their water is running out.

Two days later they are walking the same narrowed bush when the path begins to widen. Suddenly it opens up to a wide dirt road which cuts diagonally across it. They stop and the man looks up the road, right, left, right again. He withdraws his scrap of card from his trouser pocket and studies it. Glancing up at the far-off terrain his eyes settle on a distinct conical hill swabbed with the dark greens of trees. They turn onto the road and the cart straightens up on the level turf and goes careening forward with the ease of a locomotive skidding along iron rails. They move along swiftly, all prodding towards the inkling of some great twist of fortune around the bend.

A road this wide, smoothed and graded, must lead to some place that appears on a map, to some area accounted for in the known world. Beside them there are signs the virgin veld is thinning and then there is the sight of low rutted fields knitted into the land. The cart leaves a fine russet spray of bald soil in its wake. Eventually they come to a fork where a pole is pegged into the ground. Across its top is nailed a sheet of wavy tin pointing up the road and in faint ochre letters some legend is inscribed. They stop and scrutinize the lettering and run the words over their tongues. The man stares up the path of the road and trains his sight again on the distant landmark cone blaring like a hazy tower against the starched blueness. They press on up the road.

They rise some and then dip again and at times it's difficult to lug the cart uphill. He feels weaker and weaker. When they climb the slight ridges, the veld on the right thins and they are given a glimpse of the lands below. In the distance the square patches of fields stand out starkly against the yellowed flush of the bush. His eyes are blunt and he can't see well. Further on, the road angles sharply and the boys go scouting ahead. Soon the man leads them off at a tangent into the bush. The cart strains to part the dense grass; the boys have to heave from behind and lift it off its wheels. They plough through the scrub and the flange of grass and he almost stumbles over his own feet. They cut across a flush sector while the road skirts round them and after a time they come to an abrupt halt. There is a tall security fence, knotted atop with gnarled coils of barbed wire. The boys stagger forwards to part the grass and open up a window with a wide view onto a sprawl of farm buildings close before them.

The farmhouse nestles in the wattled shade of tall pouting trees, their fissured bark rough and grey, their pods flat and kidney shaped. They are exotic anomalies to this landscape and stand out more prominently than the house itself, which is long and low and flat with a red tin roof in places rusted brown in runs of flaky bronze. A veranda runs along its length with low squat Spanish arches. The windows are all closed, the curtains drawn, the dense mosquito gauzes ratcheted tight. Even from a distance a wide and uncompromising desertion of the place is tangible. A truck stands in the yard bricked up with its bonnet open, its oily innards stripped and heaped about. The browning lawn has grown thick and weedy, the tawny flowerbeds dry and drooping in the sun.

Adjacent to the house is a fenced courtyard and in it some dogs lie against the muddy soiled walls. Their tails whip tirelessly at the flies. One shakes its ears. Another hauls itself to its feet and limps over to the fence, staring half alert in their direction. The old habits that die hard. A quick shiver runs across his aching spine. It's a black dog, its rack of ribs moulded through its sleek coat. Skin and bone and barely alive. It glares at them and pricks its ears up and then trails off, flumping to the ground. The man watches the dogs for a while. Possibly he is thinking: what is keeping them alive? Or: who is keeping them alive?

The man reaches behind him, grips the butt of the rifle and swings it off his shoulder. The boys take their cue and unsheathe their machetes. They move off to the right, stalking along the bush like bandits, a pride behind a herd. This is a vain attempt to silence their progression when every roll of the cart's wheels over the scrub crackles and bristles. It makes them seem ludicrous. They creep along an arch of bush, along the hem of the fence until they have come almost full-circle. Again the boys part the grass and the man kneels down and trains the rifle barrel through the fencing. There is a huddle of outbuildings before them, at the back of the house. A workshop, then a series of coops and sties. In the coops a few fat hens wobble and flutter. In the sties lie some goats gazing out across the diamond-shaped wire and into the encroaching bush and the wild afield.

They stare in wonderment at the goats and hens for a long time. It seems like an illusion, or some cunning trap. They stay there, lowered and readied, the man looking through the scope of the rifle at every sector of the yard, probing every hollow, every deepening scar of shade. Then he sits up. Then they move off, back through the bush, trampling the pink-haired spikelets of the grass and clawing their way towards the yawning sight of a clearing that lies ahead, off to the right. They stoop down as they approach the bare pitted redness of the earth and then stop altogether. They cower and scan the openness. Beyond there are the thatched tops of huts, mulched grey and neatly fringed, almost swallowed by the spread of a stubby tree with dark corky bark and an umbrella spray of coral-red flowers. They look on intensely, every muscle stiff and straining.

The compound is deserted. They inch forwards and begin to delve into the huts one by one. They yield little of value: a few pots, some tatty fabric, some utensils. All else was cleared out when the occupants fled. There is a fire pit with cindered logs and a pool of cinder ash. Then, from round the back of the huts, one of the boys calls out. The man steadies his rifle and stalks forward. But the cry isn't one of fright or horror. They all shuffle round and ahead they see the boy waving at them, leaping up and down like a child at play. The wave of excitement hits them. They almost don't know how to respond. Away from the huts and a small way into the bush there is a clearing and in the centre of a clearing a black well plunges deep into the earth.

They work the hand pump eagerly. It squeaks and hisses. There is a running grumble that slurps deep from the guts of the well and water suddenly gushes from the tap. They each sate their thirst one by one and repeatedly.

He stands there looking on. His sore mouth salivating. He senses he will get his chance so he doesn't panic or grow impatient. At last they unhitch the cart and he goes stumbling forwards and begins to drink his fill, lapping at the tap for some minutes. His parched throat thaws and his stomach bloats until he is close to retching. The containers are filled to the brim and then they sit about and rest. The relief is so tangible it's as if each of them has shed ten years from their slack, wearied bodies.

A short while later the boys strip naked and wash themselves from head to toe, cupping water into their palms and dousing the grimy filth from them until once again their skins shimmer with that black slippery sleekness. They look like the oiled bodies of seals. The man follows them. The woman rinses their clothes in the water, scrubbing them in her hands before wringing them out and spreading them in the sun to dry. She strips too, unashamed of her fulsome breasts, the nipples swollen and gibbous, draped over the tight stretch of patchy brown skin pulled around the sphere of her belly. They wrap sacks round their waists as loincloths and bask in the eclipsing shade of the huts. Even the rifle stands cocked up against the mud wall, the belt of bullets draped on the ground, away from the man for the very first time.

So the afternoon lies supine before them, a long and languid lull that is alien to their lot. Here they are just five figures knit in a capsule of space and time, cocooned in the bliss of ignorance, spun out of nothing but the air on their breath, the water running through them. They curl in the sloping shadows and sleep away from the glazing sun. For this short time it's as if they are bereft of everything that has gone before. If any one of them were to wake now, stagger from their bedding and stand in the amber dusk light, they may fail to place the last hours and days of their ordeal at all. It would be like a benefaction, something they could never know and would hardly understand. In this momentary absence of blood and bullets, booms and bodies, all is a lucent space, something akin to the whiteness of the far sky or the fineness of pooling water that blinkers their vision. Even the rope that ties and binds him during this time becomes nothing but an illusionary figment. When the night comes they rouse themselves and sit under the spume of stars waiting for the encroaching spores of reality to catch up with them again.

L ate in the night he hears the muffled whispers burning about him and movement and footsteps trailing off into the bush. He doesn't stir. He lies there listening to the night-time sounds: the close scrawl of a cricket sprouting a lone soliloquy accompanied by a dull faraway lowing.

The others return soon, pulling something through the bush. He can hear the thrush grass bending and the swish of a weight being dragged across the slippery stalks. He raises his head and focuses his eyes and sees them grouped round the grizzled remains of the dead fire. The boys are kneeling over some form-less matter, hunks of black heaped on the ground. Then the form becomes the shape of stiff legs, tipped with the silhouetted cleft of hooves, and a neck arched back. It's the body of a goat lying slack before them. There are three in total and in a clutch beside the goats are some hens, the necks lopped, the heads tossed away. Speedily and quietly the boys work with their machetes and a small knife. They gut the goats, tearing at the inside of the skin, drawing it back to discard the innards. They heap the viscera aside and it sits there like some dark gelled accusation. The boys pool the black blood back and forth between the skin and the flesh and drain it into a pot. Meanwhile the man sits plucking the feath-ers from the hens and in no time at all their shiny pink skin glows plump under the deep night stars and the orbed moon that has now arisen.

They cannot see well but they make the progress of skilled

butchers. They break apart the limbs of the goats, hack at the joints, splice the flesh. Soon the carcasses are nothing but hollowed-out shells, scaled down to naked bone and cartilage. They dump them aside in the bush. All that's left are the piles of meat – clean, odourless, fresh – which they sit before now in silence and at rest.

The man scoops up the pot and hands it to the boys and they drink from it in turn, sipping at the rich darkness of the blood which stains their lips and teeth and dribbles a bit down their chins before they lick at it or swipe it with a finger. Warrior boys at some ritual initiation, streaked and marked for battle. They stack the meat atop the sacks and in the metal bowls. Some of it they pierce with hooks shaped from a coil of wire and hang it from the trees to bleed out. Then he drifts off into his blanking detachments again.

In the morning there it is all about them in the quivering grey of dawn like an excessive promotional display in a deli. There is something surreal about their luck and its sudden excesses. What will they do with such a bounty of meat before the sun rots it through and the flies suck it up?

The woman wobbles from her mat and cooks them up a feast for breakfast. The fire is restacked and lit and soon the hooks of meat dangle in the smoke and brown and blacken over the embers. They sit about and gorge themselves, chewing and slobbering at the meat, a pack of cannibals after a pre-dawn hunt. He has no taste for it. It repels him. The smell of it cooking sends him bilious, the sight of it makes him want to heave. He sticks with his own food and plain as it is he gets by on it. There is a lot more to their clutter this morning. In the night they have managed to loot an assorted bundle of clothes, a few pillows and blankets, some empty glass milk bottles and some Tupperware boxes from the farmhouse. Some cutlery too. After the meal they sit about salting the meat vigorously with a salt-shaker.

They drink their fill again from the well. Each one in turn and he last of all. They fill all the containers to the brim and stack them on the cart. The chassis slumps, the axle sags. Once they have finished luxuriating in the water the man sets about dismantling the well pump. He sits there bashing at the parts with the butt of a machete until bit by bit the pipes come loose and the nuts, bolts, springs, coils lie splayed in the sand about him. Meticulously he picks them up, shakes out a plastic shopping bag from one of the sacks and deposits the parts, wrapping them up tightly to store away.

They press the salted chicken into the Tupperware. They unhook the slips of goat meat from the trees, strip long thin branches and tag the hooks on each end to balance it out carefully. There are three altogether. The slices of meat are crammed on full until the sticks bulge and bend in the middle. Then they rip some sheeting and bundle the sticks across the backs of each of their necks, himself included. They look like cattle or oxen with braces fixed to them. The meat bobs about to and fro on the hooks still bleeding. When the sun rises full the salt will dry it out and preserve it and in this way they will have meat for a good few days to come.

They gather the rest of their wares. The man slings the rifle over his shoulder and straps on the belt of bullets. The woman is eased into the cart. They have to keep moving for her sake. They pull themselves away from this place and the well. It is not easy. He senses their reluctance. Perhaps he feels it most keenly, his legs heavy as they lead him off, rooted deep in some purling vein. His brain well stemmed in the emollience of it. They peel away and curve off from the compound and ease back onto the track.

They follow the road from the compound which weaves and arches, drawing near the tall security fence of the farmyard. With their bellies full and their bodies cooled, their minds may be doused in their good fortune, their guard lowered. As they curve onto the road leading them away from the farmyard a human call breaks over the morning thrum and a figure in blue overalls comes jogging up the road behind them, carrying a staff. He calls and signals them with his hand to slow and wait. His attempt to look urgent is pathetic.

They draw to a halt and the man slings the rifle from his shoulder and strides forward, calling back. The blue figure slows to a spindly walk, his hair steel coloured, the wiry silver curls of his beard bristling starkly against his gaunt, puckered face. His eyes have sunk deep into his skull and through the unbuttoned overalls his bare chest, ribbed with a bow of bones, glares out. He grumbles between short gasps of breath and points with the staff at the farmyard and at the racks of meat they carry. He spits with rage and the man listens to his ranting for a time before stepping forward and slugging the butt of the rifle into the man's temple. It cracks against his skull like a whip. The farmhand falters back on his feet and keels over in a slight swell of dust. There is a moment of raw fright between them all. The rifle butt is still raised and they all look on at the body heaped on the ground. A neat rivulet of blood seeps in the silence down his temple, dripping into the soil and staining it.

The man shouts for them to move on and they walk forward, stiff with shock. There is little conversation from any of them after this; little that resembles their former ease. The boys stalk forward, weary on their feet. The ever-stoical face of the man shows no glimmer of remorse. He is, as ever, hardened, resolved. The woman slumps down in the cart, turning herself away from the day and its actions. She lies there quiet and petulant. All this is for her, in a way. The deeds of man and his desperation. They trudge on up the road and away from the farm, rejoining the narrow path that snakes them off into the thick smothering bush once again. They plough on, the heat notching up, a scourge breaking over them at midday.

So in the heat they wind away through the plush bush. When they are tired they stop and drink and when they are hungry they pick at the dangled railings of dried meat and gnaw on it. Often they stop because the woman is ill or she has been wailing in pain. There is now little shade out here: the trees are sparse, bare, whittled down, all staggered away from the line of the path. To compensate the vlei grass grows tall and barbed, with sheaths that are keeled, awns that are spiked and tinctured a burnt gold. As they pass through its arching passages it itches and irritates them, stinging their eyes. They get tired of hacking at it. Sometimes the racks of meat get tangled and they have to dislodge them from their necks and carry them aloft. Other times they skim the tops of the tassels effortlessly.

But the passage each time is fraught with an edgy tension: they want to know what awaits them on the other side of the screen. Once he thinks he sees the brown bulk of some mammal streak the deep undergrowth beside them but he cannot be sure. Glimpsed above them all the while through the wreathed over-hangs is the clear blue sky, the faceless dome under which they crawl. Some senseless depth the mind cannot reconcile. Seldom a cloud is posted in the sky. Never a hint of rain.

The further they go from the city – such a distant memory now – the more hostile, the more alien everything becomes. He has still to discover the purpose of their travels or why it is they ensnared him. All along the journey the gun has been a constant worry to him, a force of threat and terror. His instincts stretch to the vague understanding that once they have dispensed with his services they may dispense with him altogether. He fears this more than anything. He is aware that he is only a slave tied to his services. A thin thread that may be, the weakest of attachments. He may become a liability. He may have no further chore to undertake. Nothing more to pull. But how his mind will flinch when the AK47 is cocked at his temple or his neck at the end of all this, his ears anticipating the catastrophic blast?

Perhaps they will spare a bullet, but hack into him with the machete, slash at his chest till his heart gives way and his brain goes blank? Maybe they will strap a bomb to his back and send him walking into a crowded village or small town full of militants to clear the way? Or they may sell him or use him to barter when the food finally runs out. Then what will be his fate? Sold on to the next journeying terrorist, guerrilla soldier, rebel leader? So the ordeal can start again, this mind-swept hell. Escape has crossed his mind many times even though it's impossible. Where would he go? Out there? He would last a day. Maybe two. The sheer loneliness of the bush, the infinite solitude of freedom would probably finish him off. He would be a real captive then, tied to his heartbeat, chained to the slavish paranoia of his mind. The open plains would be his den. The wide savannah his prison cell.

The truth is that he's often too tired to think about it. Often he just wants to sleep, not caring sometimes whether he wakes again or not. Even the mosquitoes would struggle to keep him awake. Even the distant fear that hounds him, the contingency of fright frizzling on in the distant reaches of his dulled, sun-bashed brain. He presumes the rest of reality drones on in a hazy reel which he senses with a certain quivering dread may not be real at all. And one can't do much – not eat nor drink nor rest nor plan an escape – when one is forced to walk and walk as he's forced to, those long trudging miles with no end in sight.

The end of yet another day. Another day which may be one or many days; in which they may have travelled far or not at all. They come down the side of a kopje through a tall stagger of beige bush and into a clearing of sparse scrubland. A red pool of dust. Clomps of weedy grass scattered in tufts like islands. They come to a halt and here it seems they will settle for the night. Here where the sun smashes into the sleek sides of a scarp and shards of copper light fall in steep decline down the sides of a ravine. The boys as usual are tasked with hacking down firewood and build-ing the fire. The man maps out who is to sleep where and who is to stay on guard. They eat a little supper: half a tin of baked beans, slivers of relish, slivers of the meat.

In the distance the sun plunges and blazes a weakened red, then an intense orange. He couldn't say this evening that he is too down-hearted or unhappy. Or even terribly afraid. Rather his fear has settled down into a blunt edginess. So the evening sits for a while, then night comes. The bonfire spits and roars and from the tree where he's tied he looks on in strange wonderment at the glowing embers for no other reason than to think they're dancing in his eyes. He beds down to the naked night where above them the spills of the firmament trawl and blinker. Births of some reck-oning that are relations to them all, seeded from their inner selves, the ever deepening spawn. Out there labour is eternal. Slow, huge, cataclysmic. All things are atomic and evolutionary and univer-sal. Out there a star is born and here a child will be its cosmic sibling. All is the purest iron.

The meat dries but the pieces that weren't salted through begin to turn grey and stink. Flies crust in on it. The airy stench is unbearable. He feels nauseous and his stomach is queasy. He grows weaker still. He can feel his bones decalcifying from the inside out; he can feel his muscles harden into knots, his skin slacken round his thinning torso.

Finally they resign themselves to the loss of the meat. They pull off the rotten pieces and throw them to the bushes, cursing the misfortune of it. The chicken they devour quickly, fearing the same outcome. They break it into pieces and skewer the flesh over the fire. The meat is scorched and blackened so there isn't a trace of moisture left swimming in it. When it is done they draw it off the skewers, pull it apart with their hands and bite into it. They turn it in on their tongues and chew on it.

Their bellies are full of poultry and they each have a dram of water. They set off early in the grey breaking glow and have made good progress by the time the sun is full over them. The air is cooler first thing and not so humid, not so sapping. There is an inkling of a westerly current strident above them, but by late morning there is no trace of it. The heat stalks back and they begin to tire. His feet hurt and his head pounds. Finally late in the afternoon they near a clearing in the veld. The bush thins to scrub and then to a bald clearing of smoothly polished sod circled with logs. Some gathering place. Some site of ritual and worship.

They crawl on through the flange and beyond the clearing the path winds a further distance until eventually the veld thins again and the tracts of cultivated land ease into the panorama. But the fields are bare and ropy with weeds dried crisp beneath the summer's scorn. He looks across the plains where there is an arc of low stubby trees and nestling just beyond them is a ring of huts fused with the rufous glow of the soils and the beige thatching of the bush. Their step quickens at the sight; the prospect of rest and shade edging them on.

When they get closer he begins to realize that something is amiss. At their helm he sees the man's breath deepen and caution enter into his step. They follow in his wake, slowing their pace. Even from a distance the silence and stillness of it throngs the stale day. From just beyond the hem of trees he sees the air quivering, sheets of blackness bending and billowing in the low altitudes. Then he registers the swarms of flies, the low seething hiss zapping the air like some electric surge. They hardly dare put one foot ahead of the next. Behind him he's aware of the woman listing sickly over the side of the cart, gripping onto the edges of the cab. The boys fall back. But the man pulls on the rope so it bites into his neck. His legs strain, the harness tautens and so their lolloping contraption gets jolted along regardless.

The smell. Another few paces onwards and it swamps them unawares on the back of a slight furl that sweeps down low over the compound and careens towards them. At first like some rotting fetor the brain knows no similarity to, some alchemy of the sun and the air combined. Then like the stench of offal thrown to the cesspit days ago. The others mask their faces with their hands but he is not so lucky. The reek hits his stomach; he belches and stumbles forward to the awaiting horror.

The dead lie littered over the clearing, like something in an epic poem of horror and damnation. It is a sight the eyes are almost unable to encounter or register. The forecourt is slaked with viscid blood, drying rivers of some quick and frenzied holocaust. They lie fallen to the laved earth; their skulls cloven grey and raw, the mutilations of their gutted bodies too incomprehensible to fathom, unravelled to the orgy of flies festering and sucking in a fevered pitch. There is no ground deprived of a corpse and no place the eye can land without visiting a slew of bodies. Like prized trophies dumped from a day's hunt in the wild. They stand there some time, seemingly fixed to the ground, to the aberrations that draw in their stares.

The reality is something that paralyzes them, throwing off their sense of awareness of the known world. The sun has grown weaker in the moments they stand there, paler as if in its own solemnity. Soon it will go down over this death scene. Time will file the edges; the coming wind and heat and rain and the saprophytes will do their bidding, gnawing at the flesh, picking at the skin, bleaching the bones whiter, whiter than light.

Finally they pick their way around this cemetery and stagger off towards the nest of huts behind it and then onwards to the vacant kraal. The ghostliness of it. Each tub of a hut squatting in the stillness and the silences of the great vacancy that has sated them. Doors ajar to dark interiors. The disjointed function of their emptied states. Fragments of spirits hankered in the deeps. The man and the boys venture forward and probe each one. The woman and he remain stationary outside. As the sun slips away and the light mellows he feels a shiver quake his body that is no ordinary coolness breaking in the air. He tries to ignore the line of bodies petrifying behind him, except for the roam of flies that quicken their erosion and the smell that sears the mind whenever there is the slightest shuffle of a breeze.

The scavenging men upturn little of value. There is no shame in rummaging amongst the relics of the dead when one is desperate. The village has been well and truly ransacked. Only some little bits of bedding and straw mats and a clattering of utensils has been spared by the rampaging militia. No food that he can see. He stands there as they excavate hut by hut and he is tired. Behind him the woman somehow manages to disembark the cart unaided. She stands stretching her bloated body and kneading her fingers into the base of her spine, a downcast look on her face. She wobbles off behind the nearest hut and he listens for the gush that accompanies her ablutions. He feels his mind drift off to some place where the grizzly tension that haunts his sight and scalds his brain doesn't goad him. The men come back clutching their finds, staring beyond him at the open cart. They look to one another. Evidently she has been gone for some time.

They scout the kraal and the huts and the fields. They are tired just as he is and mutter and curse the annoyance of it. He is left standing there with the cart attached, unable to sink to the ground. He breathes hard into the curling air and waits there amongst such visions of the dead that he hardly knows. There are moments he would envy their restive poise, freed from drudgery and the shackles of existence.

Eventually they come trailing back, the boys dragging the woman between them, her feet carving a wake of dust behind her in which the grainy figure of the man strides, flailing her feet and legs at random with the butt of a branch he has hewn from a tree. He sees the streaming anguish run down her face, the clear channels of tears wash between the dust on her cheeks. Her mouth is wracked in the spasms of her screams that sour the declining day. They drag her towards him and he stands watching it all, a neutral spectator at some ancient ritual.

The man continues to lash her and she yammers and wails at each strike. They pull her into one of the huts and the boys fall away panting whilst the man goes into the darkness after her with the stick. He hears the thuds and shouts reverberate and his own heart quicken in his throat. The boys hang around peering on, each with the look of raw sickness. When the man breaks free from the hut he throws down the stick and comes striding towards him. He can smell the rage of this man. He ought to bolt now before his captor reaches for the rifle and sticks a bullet in his skull. He shudders on his feet and clenches his eyes but the man walks right past him and fiddles with the sacks on the cart, rifling amongst the clutter to unearth a stretch of the rolled wire. He walks back to the hut and scrapes closed the door across the formless whimpering of the woman, wiring it shut so tight there is no beast in the known world that would breach it. He stands before it and looks on for some moments. He walks round the hut and kneels against its baked walls and rests his head in his arms, heaving breathlessly and looking up at the unheeding sky and dropping his head again to his arms. The boys stand cowering. No one moves for a good time. Gradually the light falls dimmer and greyer over this fractured scene.

The boys compose themselves and set about the business of a camp. They undo the harness and the weight of the cart falls from his shoulders. What a relief that is, as if a boulder on his back has been dropped to its rightful place. He staggers off towards the walls of the nearest hut and breathes deeply. His vision swims and

the ground wavers beneath him and the events of the day fluctu-
ate, a gyre swivelling in his mind. The boys clatter round him and
move him off to the far side of the kraal where they are screened
from the bodies which had been wilting away into the coming
darkness. No redness in the sky this dusk. Just the blinking scar
of the distant horizon beyond the fields and the bush stretch and
the ruddy effluence of the day spilled skywards.

The man at last picks himself up and comes along to their station, busying himself with the boys. They unravel their wares and
pile some kindling, striking a single match to light the fire which
pulses dimly like some singular stroke of life out there, at the end
of this day. They huddle about it wearily. The boys may as well
be old cripples nursing the ills of time. The man is quiet except for
the odd groan, perhaps in response to some perpetual haranguing
of his tired, faltering mind. He presses his body against the coolness of the kraal fencing and lets the slated walls rub against his
muscles and bones. He hunkers down and his aching limbs fall
numb and his spine is very sore.

The woman is to remain locked up all night. Like a grounded
child she gets no supper. She cannot be heard but he presumes she
whoops still, coiled up in the dark confines of her vault. There are
probably no rags or bedding for her to rest on. Such is her lot.
They pick some meat off the racks and chew on it. They delve
into the sacks and produce a couple of maize cobs. The boys
skewer them and char them over the flame. The man chews
through one and the boys share theirs sulkily. He gets nothing,
just looks on disconsolately. The cobs are too precious for him.
Perhaps in his own detached way he understands this too.

Once they have supped they rest against the walls of the hut, slumped there, three tramps at the slag end of a day without mercy. At a place where the small things matter so much, the very rub of existence. Finally, one of the boys slumps over to him and undoes the gag, loosening the ropes a fraction from his raw neck. He is given some water; they may not know the value of their lives but they know the value of an asset.

After this he sleeps well enough for a time. When the wind rises in the cool early hours the stench of the corpses circles through the air and wakes him with muddied thoughts that his overtired mind cannot at once dismiss. There are no waifs of the night stalking about him. No ghouls picking themselves up from the spent ground, staggering and staring out over the barren lunar greyness, but still he is adrift in some promontory of the mind. Seconds pass of an unplaced fear, a despondency and dullness more terrifying than any haunted land. He looks about but all is still. The men have quartered themselves in one of the huts. The woman is still locked up. He is alone out here.

Dawn quivers and he glimpses the coming light. The next time he looks the fullness of day is replete and one of the boys is kicking him and pulling on the rope. He shuffles to his feet and tries to compose his waking mind to the new day. His back hurts as never before but he doesn't wince or groan. They pull him along and station him in front of the cart. The harnesses are attached in their usual custom and then they all stand and watch as the man unfastens the wire on the door and pulls it open so that a shower of light shatters the darkness of her cell. The dust motes scramble, flies scatter. Somewhere beyond that gauzy fussing is the woman and the child in her womb and the question looms of whether or not they have survived the heat and hostilities of the night.

She is battered and bruised and has oozing welts on the backs of her calves and shins, a wide suppurating cut below her left eye. Her left cheek is swollen. She limps out aided underarm by the man. Her slotted eyes look glassed and embittered but she is supple enough in his grip to allow him to install her once again in the cab. The crusts of yesterday's tears lie on her face like scars; in the daytime glare they now unclot, slacking the dried blood of her wound into a fresh stream. She mewls softly, her head droops down across her chest. The welts on her shins and calves will bulge, ooze, puss over. Scabs will soon form hard, sealing her flesh. Her face will heal when the gash dries into her skin; the swollen cheek will recline to the bone. She will be okay.

They load up the sacks, wedge the water containers between her legs and off they trundle once again. The cart lolloping along as ever, its two fat wheels branding the fine soil with their tread, some mark at least that they have come and gone. Weaving past the kraal and through the huts, they move away from the line of corpses now surrounded again in the daylight by a clustering orgy of flies. They ease their way through the fields, back onto the path and walk the hard unending land again. They inch along it. Its rusted soil, the scabby tufts knotted to the turf. The vlei grass that is a weak green in the morning glow, sweet with dew, and livid at noon when the parching sun closes in, scorching everything.

The slog as ever is arduous in the unbending heat. The changing folds of land. The bush thinning; the outcrops rising; the kopjes saddled with stubby, reticulate trees. Then the semi-arid terrain. He has never in his life seen harshness like it. A drought has visited this land and the veld here is so dense and impenetrable it's as if iron spokes have been forged in the bowels of the earth and pushed through. He has never tread rocks as hard or brazen. Rocks cast from the same plutonic spurt as the vlei, metal cased and glass sharp. The distant scarp walls stagger round them like Gothic monoliths, rending a dull echo as they file through them bit by bit.

Out of the valley and across the plains they tramp. In the distance another low ridge rises, staggered against the frieze of blue.

Conical, bulging, slowly sharpening. A row of dykes soon snakes before them. The path leads nowhere but onwards to its cobbled base. Upwards they go. They surge the scarps and he battles to keep his footing on the shards of rock, the narrowness of the passes. They unbundle the racks of meat and stack them in the cart and the woman is aided; the man takes her and helps her hobble on. It's impossible for the cart to wheel up such terrain so the boys unlatch the harness and take control. They have to steer the cart between them, one pulling, the other pushing. They angle the wheels and lift it, heaving at the chassis. Somehow they jangle forward. They toil like this for a while, like some great wounded beast lugging its dying hulk up into the caves to sleep. Then the right wheel lodges in a boulder. Both boys push and strain. From under them the boulder disintegrates and dust billows up: the cart topples sideways in a plume and veers down the ledge.

The sound is unnatural and jars the ear as the cart cascades downwards. The sacks and provisions splay far and wide. The man turns and roars in panic, the boys are already shimmying down the scarp after it. The cart smashes into a lean tree and bolts sideways and is caught amongst the claws of thick scrub. It rests there still and empty. The boys reach it in no time. It has not fallen from too far a height. The man picks his way down soon after, looks over the wreckage and falls back against the side of the ledge, burying his head in his hands. The boys look at one another. The cries of the man plummet down the spree and reverberate off the low boulders. A sad whimpering plaint bells out about them.

They spend the remaining hours of daylight scratching and clawing at the incline, its scars, hollows, lees. The cart is intact as far as he can see but its left wheel is severed and the axle looks bent.

They dig the missing wheel up from the undergrowth and the man sits about the wreckage trying to fathom a way to repair it. Not easy without tools. Finally one of the boys combing the scrub unearths the coil of wire. The man sets about mending the wheel with wire and flint and some spokes of wood that they splice with the machetes. He bashes at the bent axle with rocks. He needles the splints into the sockets and wires them tight to the under-carriage. How long it will last is anyone's guess.

The boys scrabble over every inch of the area and scoop together the remains of their wares. The pillows and blankets are salvaged, the racks of meat picked from the scrub and dusted, the grit picked off them with painstaking attention. But one of the sacks has burst and the millet has scattered amongst the soil; the mealie meal sifted off vaporously into the white hot air. The milk bottles filled with water have smashed against the rocks, their contents long ago leaked into the gravel. The Coke bottle too. The larger of the water containers toppled and rolled, but with luck its top held firm. The boys carry it back up the dyke like a holy relic.

Then one of them finds the shopping bag filled with the parts of the dismantled well pump. Meticulous as ever the man undoes all his work on the cart and using bits and pieces he sets about fixing it all over again. He spends a good two hours hunched over this chore and not one of them speaks for this time.

They heave the cart back up the crag face. It isn't easy but they do it. They spend a stark night up there on the dyke. The cool air is not unwelcome but it's lined with a frigid edge. The man sits silent, brooding, phlegmatic. The boys know they are banished so they skulk off a further way up the dyke and he doesn't see them till dawn. A little sliver of the meat is all anyone eats. He wakes in the night to the woman crying softly. She doesn't stop. Like the mosquitoes she sobs in a low drone. The man lifts his head and crawls over to her. He runs his hand over her check. He kisses her neck. Then he moves a hand down to her bulging stomach and she can hear is her heaving chest. The man crawls back to his bedding and lies down, covering his head with his arms.

They come down off the dykes sometime the following morning. The boys carry the battered cart the whole way. He just does as he's told and walks. The woman has to stop every few metres: she bends over, sucking at the air. They plumb the flatland sinks for a bit before they decide to test the cart. They lower it to the ground, attach the harness and lead him on. It lollops along ungraciously, a limping animal intent to out walk its injury. Yet it seems stable enough. The man stands observing. A slight grunt. He gestures and the woman comes over and they ease her into the cab. The left side has cracked but the back seems firm. It sags but the wheel holds. They trundle forwards.

The sun is unforgiving down there in the lowlands. It is not long before they tire, start to sweat and pant. The man pulls them along, labouring hard. He is extra cautious with the water now, only allowing them small breaks every hour. Without the Coke bottle they must pour it into the metal dish and each sip at it in turn. The dish is slimy with the dried juices of the meat but he laps at it when they leave a little in it for him and is grateful for small mercies.

They stoop on, sapped of every store of energy their bodies had mustered. When they stop now they all bend over double. One of the boys is the first to break with a stitch. He holds the side of his stomach and grimaces. Tears bleed down his face. The man pulls them on, ignoring the moaning cries of the chorus behind him.

He seems deaf sometimes to all suffering, all pain, all logic. Only when he presumes the next hour has passed does he allow the bowl to be half-filled and handed around. By then the boy has fallen some way behind and can barely walk. His hands are crippled and stiff, his mouth frothing small bubbles as he pants and sucks and pants.

Further on, the wheel buckles. The woman is jolted; she grips her stomach in pain. It seems to pass. The man shouts and curses, ordering the boys out of the way. Without wasting a moment they haul the woman from her carriage and set about another maverick repair job, clanging and battering the undercarriage. The wire is bound tightly, the splints are hammered in.

Late in the afternoon they reach a spread of thick, dark trees with furrowed bark and the bush thickens again, huddling them in. By now each footstep is a strain across every muscle, every fibre in the body. He feels the pain over him completely. Then beyond that, a numb deadening. They all collapse at the finishing posts of a tall forked tree they had sighted from afar. Its trunk is splayed like a cross, marked there in that desolate dusty boneyard of things that were living but are no longer, of souls that had lingered. Not yet in his whole life has he experienced such a thudding quake of relief.

The boy with the cramp sits shaking and vomiting the little he has to vomit. A rampant fear sits over his whole being in a grey shroud that is visible to all. The woman subdues her own afflictions this evening and tries to attend to him. She wobbles off to one of the trees, hacks at the dry bark with the knife, strips the soft pap from the inside and brings it over to the bowl where she mashes it with the butt of one of the machetes. She mixes a little water in and takes it to the boy, rolling it into tight balls in her fingers and feeding it to him. He takes it into his mouth, sucks on it and swallows; a moment later he retches it up. She kneads another ball and passes it to him. He takes it. It is some time before he can keep a mouthful down but eventually he manages to suck at all the pulp. A while later his hand falls away from his side and his eyes flicker again. His breathing calms.

That evening they strip some trees of their leaves. They gather a large bunch of them up and sit about using fine strips of bark and grass to knit the leaves together into basins the size of plates. Then they take up their machetes and slash an area of bush until they have carved out a few metres squared. The leaves are laid out atop the shorn ground and left overnight to catch the sweet dew that they hope will come by morning.

It is the worst night of all. They don't light a fire this evening, they barely eat. They just sprawl out as if dead, drifting off in the hard grass. The tree where they tie him is spindly and when he is finally allowed to crouch down to rest he finds it buckles when he tries to lean against it. His back pulses with pain. In the absence of a fire the insects move in and maul them. He hears the party tossing, murmuring, slapping at themselves but tonight he doesn't hear the woman wake up.

In the morning the dew has collected in the hollows of the plaited leaves. They tiptoe towards them and with all the concentration in the world they lift the plates from the ground, pooling the water and draining it into the container. He looks on in amazement. This little creation traps them half a cup of water. The boys are proud of their achievement but the man doesn't say a word. He's taken to sucking the dew off the vlei grass. The succulence of it his only luxury. Once sucked, the grass is not too bitter to be bitten into and chewed. In such a way he does fine without their ever dwindling strips of salted meat. What other food stuffs were lost to the dyke he cannot tell.

The only thing to do is move on. They can only press forward and not succumb to the slowly stalking menace of the wild. The land dips and the lolloping cart picks up speed as they go down into a broad plain. During the descent the wheel flops, the cart ditches into the alluvium and leans sideways. The woman is jerked violently in the cab; she clutches onto the sides to stop herself toppling out altogether. They all run to her assistance and she lies there humped uncomfortably amongst the clutter. Her hands are groping her stomach, spasms of pain zap across her face. They prize her out and right the cart.

There is a growing hum that breaks suddenly low in the sky, growing in volume until a tremendous roar foreshadows the quick jagged sprawl of blackness reeling over the land, enveloping them, careening past in a shudder. They cower down. He stands there as the mottled chopper blades low over them, listing slightly to the right and veering in an arch down over the flatness of the plain. Its growl follows in its wake and quakes through them until all is just a low battered buzz in the distance. The shape of some large bird swooping away into a speck.

The woman has stopped crying, stifled into a silent fright. The man looks on, tracking the flight of the chopper as it dissolves into the far pale hemisphere. A moment later there is another straining roar and this time a pair of choppers streak overhead to the right of them at an altitude higher than the first. The brown and grey fatigues mark them as military planes. The man looks on nervously, his eyes cast steadily to the sky. His mind is at work; doubts are rising; the fear is setting in. He swings the rifle from his shoulder, feeds in the bead of ammunition from his belt and stands there readied.

Then he orders them into action. Out here on the verge of the sparse plain he knows they are fully exposed to the next convoy that flies over. They hoist the woman off the cart and deposit her atop some of the bedding on the soil. They set about repairing the wheel once again. All three of them are fussing over it like bees about a honeycomb. They tip the packet of spare parts, unroll the coil of wire. He hammers and bangs to straighten the chassis. The splints are aligned to the sockets, threaded through the wheel and bound tight. No more choppers careen over them during this time but the air about them is still frigid in their aftermath.

They set off again. There is an urgency now that they all understand. They need to cross the plain and take refuge in the far outcrop of trees before they're sighted from the air. The chopper could swoop low pumping shots at them, knocking them off as easy pickings. They trek hard. The cart swivels and bounces behind him but he's prepared to make the extra effort. The heat surrenders to the terror that quivers through them. Their ears are pricked for the slightest murmur of an intermittent drone across the wide drift of sky. The man walks with the rifle trained to the path ahead of him and the whole savannah is in his sights. They do not stop.

The sky remains still and taut and nothing other than those three choppers breaks the solemnity of the day. Eventually they cross the plain and begin the hard ascent of the hillock. The woman gets off the cart so it's easier for him to pull. He fears the long day's slog will be the final breaking point for his back, he feels something angular protruding from his spine as if some vertebrae have come dislodged. Still he lumbers on and finally they reach the summit. The land fans wide below, bristling greenly before them.

The hillock is dense with trees and their shelter up there is at least assured. They lay out a camp for the night. They unpack what little they have left and sit about haggard and exhausted. The boys just want to fall onto their bedding and sleep. A day's hard graft, heaving at the cart to get it up the hill; today they've worked more than he has. Certainly they look the product of their labours, listless and moody and filthy. When the dwindling slivers of meat are divided up between them they decline theirs, waving it off with a look of mild revulsion. The man scolds them, chastizing their lack of gratitude, and then eats their share, making an elaborate show to mock and tempt their regret. It doesn't work.

The pain tonight feels as if it flinches deeper into his body than it has before. He wants to spit and kick and lash at them. They bind him up; they drag him along; they tie him up at night. What right have they? He is sick of it, the misery of it. But such thought is senseless when here they all are – weary, sore, downcast, moody – still a band of five together at the top of a hill out here in the creaking dark and all of them alive, all teetering on. They have lasted this long. Perhaps they'll last a lot longer. Somehow they'll do it. They don't light a fire tonight. The night falls, a black mist about them up on this summit. Then the coolness of the air swishes around them and either eases the pain he feels or compliments it – he cannot be sure. Soon the faces of the others grow smudged and thick and are finally nothing more than blackness.

He wakes in the night. He thinks he hears a trail of footsteps attempting to ascend the hillock. His mind veers from the mugginess of sleep to a sharpness that is perhaps too real after all to be more than an illusion. But he hears footsteps thud against the cobbles and slash away against the vlei, the prickly trees. He tunes his ears and listens. He thinks he is wide awake now. This is no sole wayfarer, there are at least two pairs of feet, but then the rhythm of them grows more complex, the pattern of sound more heady. There are not two of them but three or more. He listens for a long time. The noises have stopped. He looks skywards and the moon has risen and sits like a toy dangled above a cot. His heart quickens. He lies looking at the moon and next to it the brightness of a single planet aloft in the throbbing sky.

When dawn thickens there is no sign of the intruders or evidence of their passing. They all sit about and the man takes out the last cut of meat and divides it up between them. A pitiful slice is all they get. The look on their faces is of some breaking desperation. No one talks: the only sound is the creaking of trees stretching, spreading themselves to the coming day. Something slips off a rock that may be a lizard or a snake but is probably neither. Everything is dead. Up here on the hill and amongst the trees is no different to the low flatness where all living things seem to have fled the revolution.

Their lack of energy sits over them, a dry scab full over the body. The man crawls across a ring of rocks and stations himself at the edge of an outcrop, looking out over the land. He sits for some time scrutinizing the panorama as if he were waiting for some mystic message or sign from the ancestors long strung in the ether. Maybe he is ruing his lack of planning, feeling baffled at how the path has led them so awry. Somewhere below them a military base crosses their path. It has three choppers crouched down on a crescent of ground. He is fairly certain of that.

They spend the whole day holed up there, listening all the time for another squadron of helicopters. But nothing breaks the stagnancy. They tie him up again and he looks at them with piercing bewilderment. As if he has the energy to break now and run off. But his stares go unchallenged so he lies against his tree and waits. Around noon it's steamy and humid and every breath brings a vapid warmth to his tongue. His mouth feels like a kiln. They siphon out a dish of water but he's offered none. He doesn't warrant even a slurp today. He watches them drink. Then he lowers his head, closes his eyes and tries to think of times when water was aplenty and he could stride into a lake or dam and weave his way down to the murk where the reeds stemmed and he knew for those moments while his breath held out that this was the precipice of another world. The dark coolness of water took on the meaning of myth in his existence.

They next permit themselves water late in the afternoon. He watches how they pour the container and can deduce by the lightness in hand and the angle at which the man pours that the water is close to running out altogether.

His thirst turns into a pain at the back of his throat. Dry, scratchy, blistery. Late into the night he begins to feel feverish. An untraceable coldness spawns from the insides of his bones thawing outwards, gradually heating, hitting the inside of his skin in hot spasms. He lies there and waits for it pass but when it doesn't he begins to feel an impenetrable despondency break deep inside him. Some lurching terror close at hand, the feeling that some malign force is watching over him in the darkness, bringing the cold and the heat that wracks his body and mind. Ahead of him he sees the hazy outline of three tall figures standing and watching over them all. They don't move, but they are looking. He stands up and tries to wrench himself free from the rope, moaning as the panic rises in him. He feels a sudden desire to leap from the ledge and roll floundering down into where he can't be seen. One of the boys wakes and throws something to keep him quiet. He grows more edgy. The boy comes over and kicks him in the shin. He is shocked into some instant awareness of his actions, stops moaning and stands still. The boy swaggers off to his pit of rags and falls onto them. He stands looking about him. The figures have gone, bled into the inky night. He sinks down again but his raw throat keeps him awake.

In the morning when he rises his mind is clear. Placed before him is one of the grass plates. He sees the beads of dew collected between the leaves and a sheer ecstasy blanks over him. He strains forward and licks at the juices, feeling it ooze down his raw throat. The rope has been untied so he gets up and moves at once to the tufts of grass, sucking out the sap from the blades, gnawing at them for their sweetness.

Today the others have also stripped the grass and they chew at it before scrounging in the bushes and the undergrowth, hacking at the roots of trees with the machetes. They collect a gathering of grass shoots, roots and bark. Kindling for a fire is found and a pyre stacked. The box of matches is brought out. The water from the grass plates has been drained into the dish – they pour a bit into the pot and set it to boil over the fire. The woman scrapes off the dirt from the roots, peels them and dices them; the blades of grass, too. Then some leaves she has mashed almost into a paste. The brew boils away and when it begins to bubble she scoops the pot off the heat. They let it cool, then take it in turn to spoon ladles of the soup into their mouths.

After the meal the man crawls out to the ledge again and sits there looking over the spooling promontory. He sits and gazes at the open spaces for a long time. Sometimes he rests his chin on his hands, like a monk at his meditation, out there on the ledge overlooking the world. Beneath the roof of the heavens, if there are heavens. Then he makes his way back and gives the order for them to pack the cart. The boys grab one end of it each and take charge of its safe passage down the kopje. The woman is held underarm by the man and his other arm trains the rifle ahead at the openness before them. He walks free as a bird. He contemplates seizing the opportunity to break away and plunge himself into the density of the plain they approach except that he is a slave to his nerves just as he is a slave to them.

The bush is thick and the spiky coral flange of trees pokes at him as they pass, stabbing him with thorns. If any choppers were to blade overhead now the man should be confident enough that they are completely screened by this wide shield of savannah staggered all around them. Barely an hour later and the first of the boys begins to spew up, reeling off into the bush and bending over double. A few seconds later another spate comes. They stop and look at the boy retching away. They look at one another. Before long they are all kneeling in the bushes and hugging their stomachs as the spasms grip them, throwing up their innards in a spray of muck and bile. The broth. So much for nature's gifts. They can barely move more than a few paces on before one of them has to turn to the bush. They are sweating, their skin has turned pasty. Then the cramp sets in. At one point they are all lying reeling in the dirt, holding their stomachs, clenching their faces as another bout of retching comes on or the pain of the cramp notches up and strikes.

The trees provide a little shade so they all crawl off to one and take refuge to nurse their ills as best they can. There is not much they can do but sit it out. They let their bowels run and their systems flush while they get more and more dehydrated. Then a fever begins to set in. They sit there against their trees shaking and sweating and bemoaning the sun and the cold, the dark patchy figments of their blazed brains, each alone and stricken with some shaky dread hammering down into the very core of them, the nerve roots of their souls. Even so he does not avail himself of the chance to run free. He hunkers down by the cart and pants miserably. Pain quakes through him too.

The fevers don't break easily. The boys cry and moan, at times as if their bodies are possessed by the unclaimed spirits that shackle through them, throwing their innards to the bush. They call out for help but are on their own. The woman can barely open her eyes. She lies on her side in the grasses, hugging her stomach. The man has managed to pull some of her bedding from the cart and drape it over her legs. He puts some water on his finger and tried to get her to suck on it. Her sour tongue slips through her yellowing teeth but she barely has the strength to lick. The man lifts her by the arms and cradles her in his lap, stroking her shivering limbs, her flushed skin. Sometime in the late afternoon, he calls out to her, shakes her by the arm, slaps her cheeks. He prizes open her eyes which roll back white in their sockets. He lifts her limp, azoic body in his arms and draws her close and cries out in an anguished howl that shatters the spaces all about them.

Dread slips into the air. It is electric. He can feel his limbs go numb; his heart starts a slow pounding in his chest. He stands up: some force comes from beneath him and rocks him to his feet.

The man's anguish exorcises the fevers from the boys who sit up at once wide eyed, sober, startled. They look on, fright masked across their faces. The man chides them into action: they jump up dizzily, gather their belongings, throw them into the cart. Together the three of them lift the woman's sagging body and lay her in the cab and they stagger onwards as if their souls have conjoined in this one moment to bring them all the energy they need. He senses the duty falls on him to be the strongest now. He falters on along the unfailing path; the others limping alongside him; the man slapping her cold cheeks, trying to rouse her from the depths to which she's plummeted. When one of the boys falls away sick and breathless, unable to keep pace with even the slow trudge, the man shouts after him and wills him on. He straightens, flexes his limbs again, catches up. Not for an instant does anyone allow themselves a moment to consider the possible fate of the woman and the infant quivered up inside her. How they manage to get as far as they do after all they have been through is a miracle brought forth from the deepest well.

She lies slumped and lifeless. What is the point of this mad surge if it's all in vain, if the inevitable has occurred, here at the end of the world and the freakish history that's gone before them? Her hooded eyes stay shut for long periods of time without a flicker or blink. At such moments he begins to think that indeed she lies there as dead as anything that has come and gone in this world.

The path forks and without warning the man veers them sharply to the right and they canter along almost at a right angle to the path they have taken all this while. There is an uneasy shifting alignment in the journey; a pull on the body's compass, its magnetic field that perhaps directs the instinctive route towards safety. They had been so committed to their path. He doesn't like it but he bears it. Then the man's intentions become apparent: the rusty trees thin suddenly, there is a screed of crisp, golden veld, columns of tall beige vlei grass that they press forward through and rapidly break into a clearing that takes them all by surprise. They lurch to a stop. The four of them, the cart, the woman in it. All standing there on the lip of a wide tarred road, white strips of paint streaked along its centre, curving out of sight. He looks right and left. The road is empty.

They quickly reel back, shielding themselves again in the bushes. It's not easy turning the cart around. They sit down panting, resting their heads in their arms, sweat beaded on their drawn faces. They clutch their stomachs again: one of the boys quickly disappears into the bush and they hear the familiar sound of heaving and spitting. The man is crouched by the woman, dripping the last of the water from the container into the dish. He lifts her head, parts her dry mouth with his fingers. He runs a line of water round her lips. She doesn't respond. They watch the water evaporate from her skin. The man slams his fists in frustration onto the side of the cab. He looks into the white-hot air

169

with a rage that would sear a man at a thousand paces. He dribbles a bit more water onto her mouth, slaps her. Briefly her eyes
seem to roll but they can't be sure. Silence for a while. The expectant dredge of time. Then there is movement in her mouth,
though it may just be the flicker of her tongue against the dryness
of her lips.

They cannot sit in the bush like this waiting for her to die. The
boys position themselves some distance from the front and back
of the cart. They inch it out of the bush, start trawling along the
rim of the road. The boys continually signal the road is clear
either way. No vehicles come by for some time. It may be that no
vehicles travel this road now. All the better. They could never
trust a car or a truck to stop for them now. Their slim chance of
help is to reach one of the small towns pitched along the route,
find some water, some food. The road begins to dip and beyond
its falling curve the sun is already set low in the distant horizon;
the filmy light begins to wane and weaken. A few minutes later
the boy at the rear of the convoy starts waving and shouting.
Immediately they trail off into the bushes and hide themselves
behind the ledge of bush. They wait though they cannot afford
to.

They hear a low rumble growing but they can't see anything.
The roar gets louder: a congregated clatter, the straining chug of
diesel engines. Then the first of the battery swoops past them. A
grey-brown lorry mounted on tall fat wheels; they see the clutter
of the chassis; the engine mounted below and the dark massive
underbelly of it. They cower down. It's not easy for him. Fortunately
the bush is tall and they have managed to duck down in a small
ditch.

Another lorry trails past. Then another. He sees a curious cargo on the back of them: two soldiers are stationed at each end of the carriage, sitting there in the breeze, the barrels of their AK47s pointed to the sky. Huddled beneath their watch are the packed bodies of a cluster of bare-chested boys. There are at least fifty of them, staring at the lone bush they pass, the unyielding sky, sewn together at the necks by yards of steel wire. Their tonsured heads are polished slabs of blackness refracting the dimmest orange glow of the falling sun.

The trucks thunder past. There are three of them altogether. They watch each one loll by with its terror-crazed cargo: boys looking outwards on an unknown destiny. The boys in the bushes are looking back at them. When they have trailed off into the distance they creep out of the veld and begin their trek again. The boys at each side, watching the road. The man walks beside the cart, talks to the woman, pleads with her to open her eyes, gather some strength. *We have no water left,* he is perhaps saying to her in breathless pants, *no food either. We are all sick and weak and sore but we have come a long way. We have come a long way for you and as long there is a tremor of a heartbeat in you and as long as the baby lies there we'll walk on.*

They walk on. They will walk that darkening slip of road until they happen on some instance of hope and salvation.

The evening comes over them, furling and thickening around them like a gas, miasmic and toxic. There is some portentous reckoning in the air. Their lives poised on a knife edge. The night falls soon after and the insects come out along the road. They don't hear another car coming. They don't see in the distance the stark fusion of headlamps specked into darkness and so they carry on all the while. Straining and limping, each one of them haunted by pain, withered with weakness. The moon rises low and yellow; the slate-black air cools and for a while it gives them some momentum. Then a star appears beside the moon as it always does and always will while the living have eyes to see it. An icon of the vastness and smallness of being. He registers it briefly and they carry on walking.

Up ahead in the darkness there is a furling blackness that gradually takes the shape of something squat and solid. At first he thinks it's a figment born of the dark, the tired, stolid mind. But the others register it too. They stop and wheel the cart into the bush and crouch down to scan the area. They can see nothing: just a shape hooded in black, stencilled against the night. They crawl on, tracking the tall grass. Slowly the angular form of a building takes shape. Then they see some more beyond it. There is nothing else they can gauge. Everything is quiet, formless, looming. Static and stagnant in space and time. There is not a light up on the stoep of the building, or those beyond it. No wan candlelit pulse or the blur of hurricane lamps. They creep closer, stop and look. The man is thinking hard, his eyes steeled on the prospects of what this clutch of civilization has to offer. He mouths instructions to the boys. They ease the empty water container off the cart and draw their machetes and skulk forward. Two slim beings slip from the silence and slowly steal into the broadness.

They leak out of sight. The man looks on with atavistic tension. A long time passes in which they see nothing and hear nothing. The only movement is the slow lithic fracturing of the air. His tired eyes strain to glimpse what is real against his doleful mind. The woman is still, silent in her cot. He's sure she has not uttered or grimaced since the night fell. The man holds her flaccid hand and squeezes it and doesn't let go. There is nothing he can do now. All his energies are invested in the boys and their mission.

After a while the man slides the rifle from the cart and trains it over the dark blobs of the buildings. They hear something shatter in the distance. It may be the glass of a windowpane the boys have smashed or it may be nothing other than the climatic shriek of the stillness that has finally splintered over them. He looks on and the man looks on too, his body erect and readied.

Nothing happens for a long time. Then ahead of them there comes a shuttle of lights and a dark vehicle sweeps by and skids to a stop outside the building. Grey dust unravels around the headlamps and all is blanketed in a lunar haze which hangs thick for a while over their stunned minds and over the night before atomizing into the metallic shape of an army jeep. Three soldiers get out brandishing torches that probe the stark brick of the building in fidgety beams. They start forward. He can see their lank bodies and the rifles slung on their shoulders.

The man lurches forward in the bushes and trains his rifle, his heartbeat thudding against the torpid earth. The soldiers scan the area. The torchlight spearing the sides of the buildings, mining stretches of sand and gravel. They edge onto the stoep and scour their lights against the chromed, webby windows, leaning inwards to search the interior. One of them stills his torch and gestures to the other two and says something. They come together and in unison shine their torches at a designated area inside the building. The man veers forward a bit, plants the rifle and coils down to look through the scope. His hand sits flush against the trigger. His skin and muscle flinching. But he breaks his sight and looks up. He is breathing heavily. He sets his sights again and lies there trained on a soldier's chest of mottled grey and green that he can barely see. It is no good. He'd probably miss. And then what?

He pulls away altogether and sits up breathing hard. He has to muzzle his mouth with his hands his breath is so loud, so punctured with fright. He sits there and looks back at the cart where the woman lies. He closes his eyes for a second so tight the world – its evils, its sacrifices – must vanish entirely. He looks over at the buildings again but does not re-engage the scope.

The soldiers bash in the door with one short kick. They storm in and there is only the briefest sound of a scuffle. One last stand. Soon the boys are shunted out and behind them come their three assailants. The rifle pointed at them will stop them fleeing. They are kicked in the calves and they fall to the stone stoep and lie there weak and helpless. One of them manages a gibbered cry before he is kicked in the back and in the stomach with the sharp hard end of a soldier's boots. The butts of the rifles are pounded into them. They squirm on the ground. Twitching as something severed of its nerves, sliced deep down the spinal column. Soon the jeep starts up and skids away down the road and when the billowing dust settles in its vacancy there is nothing left there but the cloistered dark

The man is stone-faced now. This is what he has to be. He raises himself and turns to the woman and wipes her brow with the edge of the bedding. He takes her arm and feels for a pulse. Then the man gets up and walks forward leading him on. No expression passes between them. Nothing between captor and captive that indicates an easing of their union, a final acknowledgement of their dual martyrdom. That they are after all both victims of one and the same system. He pulls on the rope with one hand, the other gripping the rifle, and they go staggering forward out of the bushes.

The man leads them to the buildings. He follows, afraid of the electric chill that still zaps the silent throes of the air. He tries to halt in his tracks and buckle but the man turns in an instant and leers at him. He stands still and calms himself. They move on slowly. The man brings them to a halt outside the stoep and here he looks down briefly at the spot where the boys were kicked and beaten, their absent bodies still somehow scorched into the spot.

The man tiptoes onto the stoep and looks about. Then he stands dead still. Rigid as a wildcat poised to strike. He cocks his head slightly. To the side of the building there is faint hissing sound. Something static, intermittent. The man grips the rifle firmly and stalks forward, edging his way to the side of the stoep. He lines himself flush against the wall and peers round it. They all know to be absolutely still. The hissing strains, weakens, strains. Then they hear the voice of a man calling out something, slow and repeated.

A pool of light inches over the gravel and grows stronger. There is the crunch of footsteps. The light breaks from beyond the wall and a figure stops dead in his tracks, raising his torch. He stands there with the cart behind him, ready to flee. The light piercing, intrusive. The blurred figure frozen behind it. There is a short catastrophic blast and another and the rifle jolts in the man's arm each time and the light shudders and wobbles and the figure hits the ground. He stands there still and waiting for the horror of the sound to reconcile itself to the reality of the night.

The man staggers forwards and looks out over the ledge of the stoep and down at the body of a man spread-eagled on the ground. Two rings of red blubber from his gut. In his hand there is a radio transmitter which still hisses and crackles in his dead clutch.

The man shuffles towards the body and kicks the transmitter from the upturned hand. He bends and picks it up: not once does the barrel of the gun leave the man's gut, dead as he is. He thumbs at it, turning the dials but the sound only hisses, dies, hisses again. He backs away from the body and brings the radio over to the cart and puts it next to the woman. He goes back to the dead man and leans down to pick up the torch that's rolled away, shining its beam tangentially into the night.

With the rifle jutting from his midriff he makes his way back to the stoep and enters the building. All he sees from the outside is the torch flare up the concrete grey walls with an orangey glow, the man's tall shadow reeling against it. There is some ransacking, a discordant din. Finally he comes out. He lugs the container the boys took with them: it is at least half full. He stacks it on the cart and moves back inside with one of the empty sacks. He comes out again with the sack dragging behind him, bulging full with something. He stashes it next to the woman and leads them on with haste. Away from the store and the sprawled body on the ground.

They move down the road, beyond the hazy unravelling of the town, and ditch into the bushes again. The man hauls the container from the cart and fumbles in the dark for the tin sheen of the dish. He tilts the container and a slush of thick dark liquid comes pooling into the dish. He sniffs it and dips a finger in to taste it. He crawls round the side of the cart and cradles the woman's head in his arms. Gently he drips the brew into her gaping mouth. The first bit dribbles away, sliding down her chin, down her neck and cupping in the hollow of her throat. He re-angles her head in his arms and talks to her, urging her to consciousness, shaking her awake. This time she manages to gurgle and swallow. Her throat bulges; the brew sidles down slowly. He repeats the process several times. He makes sure she has as much as she can take. The whole time he is whispering in her ear and chattering to himself. He rocks back on his feet, sway-ing her loose, swollen head in his grasp. He sways and he whispers and in whatever language his utterances are universal. A prayer in the night, some calling to a higher being.

After a while the man rummages in the sack the boys had filled in the store and brings out some lumps of food. It looks like dried figs, dried tomatoes, dried relish. The woman is too weak to eat them whole. He looks at her, longing for the taste of what she dis-regards, feeling it sit on his tongue and slip down his raw throat. The man sits there breaking some pieces of it up in his hands and mashing it between his palms. He mixes it in with some of the brew and feeds her some pulp. He slumps beside her on the turf and rests her head in the hollow of his neck and they remain motionless for a good while.

Over all of this he stands in his usual role of observer, seer of everything, bystander. He struggles to make sense of all that is happening to them, in the frosty vagueness of what his life is. It's as if he is always a step away from the immediate action of their saga. He is pulled along their path, shunted about in a never ending skein of confusion, in the urgency of someone else's fate. He is no interloper; too much separates them. Too much that can't be overcome. If the woman dies this night he'll think nothing of it. If the man then takes the rifle, props it up to his chest, leans forward and blows a hole in his gullet only the sound will shatter through him and then dissipate into ripples of nothingness. The boys are gone: so be it. He never could care for them. He, in his state, who knows nothing of empathy.

While they remain still he nestles down as best he can and as much as the harness will allow him. He lies there and lets the shock and exhaustion of the day fester over him. The mosquitoes are virulent out here. They swarm in and suck on them. He is sure there must be dampness or moisture close at hand.

His thirst is insatiable. When the shudder of the night's events wears off he registers a deathly, painful thirst wedge into his throat and dry him up from the inside. It frightens him. He looks over at the container and then at the bowl lying at the man's feet and wonders if there's anything left there he could lick. He stands and looks down on them, still and silent, their coupled breaths deep and shallow in a strange altruistic pairing. He nudges forward, shuffling in the catch of the harness, and leans down to the bowl. The sides are laved with a moistness, the odd scrape of tomato flesh, relish tassel. He brings his tongue to it and noses round the bowl, licking at the juice, the coolness of the steel.

Something elevates in his misdemeanour that he can't place; a faint surge of life lisping into his nerve-ends. Then the pain rockets at his head: a flat blast judders in his ears and he stumbles away. The man has kicked him in the side of the head. There is a sharp sting that burns at his cheek; his ears are imploding. He is up and from the corner of his eye he sees the man come for him again, fists bared. In the confusion and panic he lashes out and kicks back, stamping forward and trying to trample on the man's legs, crush his shins, his ankles. Only the weight of the cart and the restriction of the harness stop him going for his chest, his neck, his skull. He lurches forward: this could be his one chance. The man has fallen and cowers and cries out. But there is another cry that halts them both. He holds back, breathing deeply. They both look at the woman who is sitting up and clutching her stomach and screaming in pain. There is wetness puddled on the soil beneath her dress, burst waters from her womb.

The spasm of pain that jabs her does not come again for some while. They are up and spurred into action and ploughing their way along the road. She lies in the cart, her legs sprawled over the rims. Fear and shock are etched through her.

They pace the night-time glower of the road but even now there is paleness fusing itself gradually into the distant dark; the womb of the moon has sunk already; a first yolk of brazen light drifts absently into the horizon. The man is a flutter of nerves. He keeps looking up and down the road. He must be wondering who or what will save them now the hour has come.

After a while they see a small metallic blob astride the road, a slip of white which soon lengthens into the shape of a car. They press on towards it. There is a tall white man standing at the rear, his back towards them. He is busy funnelling fuel from a jerrycan. A few yards before they reach him he is alerted to their presence and staggers back in panic. The man is waving his arms to catch his attention, but the white man is fumbling at his boot lock and stuffing the jerrycan and funnel in. He rushes round to the driver's door and gets in. Beside them now, the man begins to call and plead. He cups his hands in a manner that is deplorable; he kneels beside the driver's window and begs, pointing all the while to the woman, miming the globe of her belly in the air against his stomach.

But the white man has started the car, its revs abrasive against the morning solemnity. In a flash it is gone, a streak dimming in the distance, the man still knelt on the ground, praying for a miracle.

He gets himself together and they move on.

Finally, just left of the road, they see a rickety sign posted into the gravelly soil and propped up with rocks. Snaking behind it is the sandy slip of a road. The man draws them to a halt. He bends over double, panting with visible exhalations of relief. There may be half a smile that breaks from his lips, blankets his face, shimmers in his eyes. The sign has a slender white cross painted on it and beneath it a name. They turn onto the dirt road and trundle on. Something about the man's attitude, his bearing, indicates a real shift in his demeanour. He chats to the woman; he comforts her. He points ahead up the winding stretch of dust as if to indicate to her the expected loom of some providential happening, some act of salvation at hand. Faith that ahead lies the end of the journey, the final destination, the route the mysterious path was always leading to. He can't be sure, but something about the inexplicable and sudden lightness of the man's gait conveys this to him. That help is at hand, that they'll make it after all.

Another contraction rips through her just before the road levels out and leads them to a low fence. Signposted at the entrance to the rusted gates is the same emblem of the cross in washed-out white, this time pasted in the centre of a rusted old plough disc. Beyond they can see the metal casing of a water tank atop a tripod, hard and ferrous in the early glinting sun. Beyond that, past another hem of bush, a cluster of low prefabricated buildings set flush against the khaki sprawl. The man fiddles with the gate, unravelling the springs of barbed wire that lock it. He pushes it ajar.

They enter and wind along the road, passing another cross, this one wooden, staked into the ground, surrounded by a bed of dead, ashen daisies. The water tank sizes into proportion and they walk on underneath its sheen. All is quiet, unmoving. The weight of stillness gravitates through him, a staleness to the place, a vacancy so palpable it thrums the morning air. The first row of buildings are completely deserted. Some stand open, others are shuttered. Inside there are glimpses of iron bed frames, low and sprung. The man begins to slow. He exchanges glances with the woman. He looks over the desolation. This is not what he expected.

They edge on in a shrill silence along the red brick and concrete buildings, asbestos sheeting across the roofs. They come to the end of the first row and stop in their tracks. Beyond them they see mounds of earth dumped in conical piles; to the left the ground falls steeply into a pit. They step forward and a huge crater opens up on them like a quarry. They can't see the bottom. Levelled to a foot beneath the lip of the pit are piles of bodies: naked, slim, sleek and black. Boys or adolescents. Each one with a slack, twisted neck. Bloodless welts across their throats. A savage mangle of limbs, torsos, heads.

The man staggers back, his mouth agape, his wide eyes scalded. He eventually turns from the gravesite and begins to scan the far tangle of buildings beyond them. He looks too. Then things fall into focus. Stationed behind a frieze of low, hobbled trees they can make out the shape of an army truck. They track their line: three of them, the last with its cab jutting out into a clearing, like the head of some carnivorous beast. Then they pick up the sight of a jeep parked outside a building. There may well be three helicopters sitting in a cleared arc round the back. Just then he sees something move along the line of the buildings. Three shapes, three men dressed in fatigues. They may be coming towards them.

The man kneels and lurches for the rifle off the cart, hauling them back along the route they came. They run across the first row of buildings; back along the path by the water tank; fast towards the gate. The woman is jolted back and forth; she cries out in pain, and lists over, gripping her stomach, the labour contractions biting into her. The man pulls them on. They exit the gate and veer sharply onto the gravel track that winds back to the main road. The jagged bush reels past them; the trees blur; the sky above them shudders. All he knows is the sound of desperation their failing feet make as they crunch the gravel. The cart has never sped so fast. The right wheel is joined only tenuously. He can feel that it isn't going to hold long.

They have no idea what or who is coming for them. They don't look back. He can't bear to think what will come roving up behind them, purling a wake of dust as high as the trees. There is a moment when he senses the notion of being hunted. Of being quarry fleeing the gathering, rollicking pace of a wild cat ranging in on him at a pace he can't assimilate, with a lust he'll never know. It is a moment of abject fright, of the purest lucidity he has ever had. He doesn't think of it for long.

They reach the main road and turn onto the smooth, soft tar and continue up along it. They cannot go at this pace for long. They'll all be in a heap on the road in no time at all. They slow to a hurried walk and the world steadies and resizes around them. There is blood drumming in his ears. His throat is tight. The woman cries out in anguished pain, retching and screaming. Her fists are knotted, her arms wrapped round her stomach, her head thrown back in a spasm. The man stands and watches. He scrunches his face against the pale ebbing heat, raging against the hopelessness of it all.

The contractions come quicker now, racking up against her every few minutes. They try to carry on but it's becoming impossible. The man drags them into the bushes; he kneels by her and talks to her. She is gasping, struggling for breath. He takes one of the empty sacks and holds it aloft over her to gift her some shade. He unscrews the lid on the container and dribbles some of the brew onto his fingers to dapple round her lips. Her brow is sluiced in sweat.

A bluish streak shoots past them on the road, the sound sucked into a vacuous rush. The man leaps up with the rifle and runs into the middle of the road. The back of a blue sedan: he takes aim as if he is some thoughtless automaton and slugs a few rounds into it from behind. Its rear windscreen shatters and it swerves from left to right in the road and back again. Fright zaps through him and his muscles flinch. He hears the skid of brakes and the car comes to an abrupt halt in a ditch beside the road. The man trails after it. The doors spring open and the blobs of beings in the distance can be seen trying to flee into the camouflage of the bush but he is quick to tag them down with the spray of rifle bullets he pumps into them. They fall in various attitudes, quick and soundless. One of them tries to pull himself up on his legs and crawl into the bushes but he is already tracking him, potting another bullet into his spine. The figure slumps forward and is still.

The man looks once to make sure none of them is moving and then runs back down the road. Watching the man, something notches up in him and tells him to run. The gun and its associations. The man and his madness. He tries to rear up and kick forward but already his old foe has him by the harness and is kicking his shins and slamming the butt of the rifle into his ribs. The blow is so hard he thinks his skin has been sliced clean open. It has: blood wells instantly. His insides reverberate in the aftermath. He stumbles on his feet, the pain blistering through him.

The man drags him by the rope and pulls him down the asphalt towards the car. There is rage in his blood now; his whole body arched and flexed; his jaw an obsidian arch of some primal determination. They go stumbling down the track, the cart and the woman behind him as always. He shambles along and when they close in on the car he sees the full spree of bodies lying beside it. The stark redness of blood against white tanned skin. A man has been hit in the head; a lobe of his grey brain sizzles across the tarmac.

The man lifts the woman from the cart, mustering all the strength he can, the adrenaline still sidling through him. He lays her on the back seat of the car, atop the crystalline scatter of broken glass that lies across it like big globules, like hail stones. Stripping the cart of the container, the sacks, the bedding, he bundles it all into the passenger seat in a mad and furious rush. He closes the passenger door, comes round the rear of the car. He brushes right past him and stops. The man looks at him, his hand clutching the rifle, his breathing stunted. His eyes are filmed over with an opaqueness that can't be forded. But the thought he was grappling with obviously fails him.

He climbs into the driver's seat and slams the door and attempts to start the engine. The car jolts forward. He tries again. It stutters and jerks. Twisting at the ignition; the car chokes but won't turn over. He tries again, sitting there bashing the steering wheel with his fists and screaming to himself. He looks out of the window, up ahead at the road. Then he twists the key again;

the engine strains and turns over; he revs it hard; black smoke billows from the exhaust and scatters into vapours. Through the back window he can see the woman's face flushed in pain but he doesn't hear her screams above the commotion. The car goes shunting forward, down the road, away from him and the empty cart.

He stands there and watches them disappear into the distance and then he looks down at the bodies lying across the road and dead in the ditch. The pain in his side comes back at him. He looks down and sees the blood weeping. He closes his eyes and feels his feet quake beneath him, his mind mildly fracture. There is nothing to do but carry on. The cart is now light and empty; it feels strange. Its presence has crudely shifted: the car already a far dash winding away from him all the while. He can feel its pull on his body, the phantom presence of the woman. He walks the trampled earth alongside the road for a while and he doesn't really know what he intends to do. Everything is suddenly aimless. Just an endless scrawl of yellowish grass streaking all about him and he doesn't know where to place his feet, where to sink his heart.

The cart is a burden without a purpose. It must be disposed of. The ropes are bound too tightly round his shoulders to simply slip off. If he walked on and on at some point – in a week, a month, a year – they may simply fray or unravel, the cart may bit by bit fall apart. The wheels will come off sooner or later; all he'll drag behind him is a raft of wood, a crank of iron. That too will slowly break up into planks and a pole.

He paces on until the road veers again and dips. Appearing in the near distance is a coned kopje standing green, hazed over and saturated with a darkness of trees. The prospect of shade that'll fall over him, a cool cascade. A trunk to lean on and rest. The ineffable notion of being lost in the vastness of himself. He

188

plunges into the bush, the cart lagging behind. It's an effort to pull it through the flange. He lumbers and pulls: his sights set on the dark rising mound before him. The trees are narrow and stubbly with weak, pendulous branches and the first few attempts he has at ramming the cart between them is futile. The trees bend or snap; a hammer of shocks splinters up his spine. He staggers along.

A short way up the slope there are two granitic outcrops covered in a coat of scabrous moss, streaked with bronzed stains of rust and water drip. Lying beneath them is a cluster of boulders, small as cannon balls, large as monoliths. He looks over them. He thinks hard about what he's going to do. Then he charges against the ledge sideways. Behind him the cart smashes against the ledge of stone. He hears the cab crack and splinter; the right wheel bounces off down the ridge; the cart sags behind him. He braces himself and charges at the next cluster of boulders. This time an intense pain surges up his spine and he yammers loudly but already the weight has snapped away from him and he falls freely amongst the rocks. The cart tilts and angles down the scarp crashing into the trees below.

Next he tries to unbundle himself from the clutch of ropes. Lying against the stones and rocks he begins to slide his back up and down, trying to hook the thickness of the rope against a sharp nook or ledge. He edges against the rocks and pushes himself hard against the rutted surface and tries to rip or fray the thread. He feels a sharp pain claw into him and then a cold sting at his flesh and he knows he's cut himself badly beneath his coat. He carries on struggling even though he is tired and thirsty and sore. At last he feels the rope catch on a claw and he pulls down hard against it and drags the tassel of rope up and down his body. The tension of the binding eases. He stands up and the straggles of rope fall away from his body. Soon it lies in a heap round his feet. He pants in relief. He lies down to rest.

He lies there and lets the pain wax up and down his spine. His ribcage is throbbing; the wound is bleeding again. But he is free at last of his burden. The sun can't entirely penetrate the wash of trees and only filters down in shafts. He realizes he is bathed in a dappling of shade. The stone he rests against is cool beneath him and doesn't cause much discomfort. Those slabs are dipped into the earth and cooled by the soils and at their core there is some mineral as cold and as dense as ice. He lies there lank against that earthly solace for some time.

A while later he is roaming the inclines and steps of the scarps and weaving his way through the trees where his senses take him. He climbs and then dips a long way. His footing by no means secure. The shards of stone beneath his feet are like quarry stone chipped and smashed by some great drill bit or crusher. Still he manages to pick his way along it. He comes down off the far side of the kopje. The vlei here is emerald-glazed, the grass rooted in short tufts which grow more prominent and there is the occasional wild flower pinned to a shoot or buttoned to a branch. He is tired and he is thirsty and he doesn't know what time of day it is.

He is looking for water. He may just happen across a stream, the same way he happened across a flowering vegetable patch in the middle of a wasteland. He goes deeper, deeper. There is a dank, lemony glow around him; he can see the fine motes of dust flaking down from the infinite tops of the trees. At last he stops and takes a rest. There is plenty of rich vlei grass here for him to feed on. If he's still here in the morning he'll suck the sweet dew from the stalks. He comes across to a small clearing covered in a carpet of thick dried leaves which crunch underfoot and will make as good a resting place as any other. He stands amidst it for a while. He looks out and down across the kopje and over the stretch of savannah quickly receding into the lapping waft of blueness. Just beyond the clearing the bush runs thick again, and beyond that is the lip of the road.

He looks up. He looks out across the plain beneath him and sees the dark patches where some clouds overhead stencil their shadows over the earth. It hasn't rained for a long time. He can't recall when it rained last.

He plods away off down the kopje, away from the trees. His wound is seeping into his grey matted hide, his spine aches. His four tired hooves are bruised and gorged and raw. He trawls through the bush towards the road. It's far easier now without the cart and the ropes. If his memory were better he may remember the days when he fled the noise of the revolution and took the quiet back roads to avoid the mayhem streaming from the city; fleeing the brash, blaring voices of the men who broadcast warnings and threats in a strange grumble. He would remember that he came across a plantation up in the hills on the city's outskirts and he lay low there for some days, rummaging around for food. He stood on the hillocks and watched in the distance the sky glaze over with weakening yellow pulses and then the settlement in the air of great towering belches of black smoke. He would remember the last time he walked free.

He crosses the bridge of veld between the kopje and the roadside and then he walks in the bush along the course of the road itself. He ambles for some time and makes good progress and with the cart unhinged he walks a great deal further than he imagined he could under that blistering sun. No cars pass, or trucks. No choppers blade overhead. Around a bend in the road he spots something heaped half in the bushes, half jutting into the road. He can't see it clearly to begin with. He takes a few more steps forward till his vision clears and he is able to see the shell of a sedan scorched black across its bonnet. Its rear is a pale blue that glimmers in the daytime glow.

He walks on in the bushes towards the wreckage. The shell of the car is smooth, the paint singed, the crisp black steel shining through in places like a mirror so that the formless stagger of bush is almost reflected in the panels of the doors. The front windscreen is intact. Heaped over the steering wheel is the body of the man, a bullet-hole wound in the side of his temple, his eyes glaring out stiff and static as ever on some distant goal. The tyres have been shot out and the rear door lies open, exposing a vacancy of space in which his mind can almost place the limp figure of the woman, lying there in the throes of childbirth.

4

19 November

Got a call from Veronica, wailing down the phone. 'Have ecstatic news, darling – we have an offer!' At once the dread ran through me. Oh God, I thought, the Chinese man, the Greek man.

'No no, from another gentleman. He's offering a lump sum transfer, but wants the deal settled quickly.'

'But no one else has seen the place,' I said.

'That's the beauty of it, darling – he doesn't want to. He's buying purely on spec & location. This is the best thing we could have hoped for.'

After I'd hung up, I sat thinking. Half relief, half sadness. A great deal of puzzlement. Still can't take it in. I'm debating whether I should pry into it a little more or just take the money & run.

20 November

Phoned Veronica back after a sleepless night. 'Look, can you give me a bit more info on the buyer?' I asked. 'Also the terms of the deal. It all sounded a little hazy yesterday.'

For once she sounded a little distant. 'I'm drawing up the contracts now, darling. Will have them over for you to sign in a flash.'

'No, look, that's taking it a bit too quickly. I'd really like to know more about who's buying it, maybe even meet them before I go signing anything away. After all, this is my family home we're talking about.'

There was a pause on the other end of the line. 'Ian, we have a deal. No fuss, no haggling. I can assure you it doesn't come much better than this. But he does want a quick deal. The offer's on the table. You know it's a bad market right now. What does it matter who the buyer is? He's good for the cash – direct US dollar transfer – you're leaving the country & you need your house sold.' Then: 'Plus, we need to make this sale, Ian, you & I both.'

I thought for a second. 'Okay. Go ahead.'

By four o'clock I had the papers in front of me. So quick, so processed, so neat. Me, Veronica & a very smart black lady, who arrived in a silver Mercedes & introduced herself as the buyer's lawyer. Lots of exchanging documents, signing on dotted lines, Veronica standing over us, fretting till the last.

'When does your client want to move in?' I asked the lawyer.

'Oh, he doesn't. This is part of an investment portfolio.'

'Right, I see. Can you tell me a bit about him?'

'I'm afraid I cannot. He wishes to remain discreet.'

'So what becomes of the house?'

'The property will become an asset to a holding company. That's all I'm at liberty to say.'

'Does this company have a name?'

'Darlings, let's just sign up & be done,' Veronica chipped in. I could see how rigid her body had become. I looked at her, then back at the lawyer.

'Right. Can I stay until the end of January?'

They looked at one another.

'I don't see why not,' she said.

Do I have it in me to care? I have the asking price sitting neatly in an offshore account. I'll be gone in two months. I'll cross the border & be out of this place for good. Do I really care who takes over my house? Whether it just sits in the name of some vague shelf company for the next five years possibly gaining value, possibly not?

I'm undecided on all the above. I'm undecided on everything all of a sudden.

21 November

Another brick dismantled, another part of the hem unpicked. My last day at school. Final assembly was bearable until we all stood to sing the school anthem, accompanied by the pipers. Wrench in the heart. Then on to the end of year staff lunch. Subdued affair. Everyone on a knife edge about the future of the school, the future of the country. Not a good year all round. Muller especially down in the dumps. He bid us farewell with a subtle hint of embitterment towards us. Loaded sarcastic comments like, 'Many of us who've tried to stretch our wings know that the grass isn't always greener on the other side.' As there were seven of us leaving not one of us felt particularly moved, I don't think. When it came my turn to say a few words I had been standing there thinking what to say. I wanted to say, 'I have no reason to be leaving you all, I've admired this school, it's been my second home, but these are unsettling times & unfortunately I can't see that I'll have a future here, being what I am, being a young white male.' Instead I just said thanks & good luck. They gave me a nice edition of *The Great Treasury of Western Thought*. It'll probably end up at Auction Express like everything else in my life.

22 November

Am trying not to think of school. Or the sale. Slept late & didn't surface until near noon. Thumbed through the shelves & spent the afternoon reading in bed. Read in snatches & dozed off for a while in languid oblivion, quite lost in those quaint & ageless worlds I'd transported myself into. Victorian London, the roaring Twenties, the frozen wastes of Russia. Finally got up around 4 a.m. Sat about in my boxers & tinkled on the piano (in bad need of tuning before it's sold). Dug out my old scores & set about trying to get my fingers to remember the patterns of the runs & chords & melodies. Have fixed myself on relearning the first movement of the Waldstein sonata. Why, I don't know. Some dive into escapism? Hit the right notes, but nowhere near up to tempo. Couldn't get a very pleasing tonal quality on the high passages either. V. impatient.

23 November

Interesting turn of events. Had a sudden unexpected text from Alicia asking me to go along with her to a recital by a Czech cellist & I could think of no reason not to. The whole way through the programme flashes of our previous relationship came to me. Has it really been four years since we parted company? Since her impatience with me snapped & she left for brighter prospects in London? Maybe it was the proximity of our bodies, side by side again after all these years. Maybe it was the familiar scent of the perfume she still wears. I recalled the almost formulaic pattern of our affair – sitting around arguing endlessly about art, politics, philosophy, rapidly getting through a bottle of red wine, sometimes a pasta dish, then always ending up in bed having urgent, animalistic sex which wasn't always entirely satisfactory, but was nonetheless a welcome outlet. The relationship in many ways more a union of souls & minds than a coupling of bodies.

The recital was something of a disappointment. A paltry fifty or so people, mostly rather elderly, scattered around that huge, cold auditorium. Hardly an electric ambiance. The poor guy went through the motions well enough & played a piece by Ravel I'd not heard before. Afterwards, Alicia said, 'Come back to my place for a bite to eat.'

I followed her home – a garden flat in one of those secure complexes. Modern, stylish, cosy atmosphere. As soon as I walked in I sensed the lashings of class & taste the girl has. A slight ache settled over me when I thought for the briefest of moments what I'd missed all these years. (What could have been?)

It turns out she has been back for some months, in fact the better part of the year. She has obviously come into some money. Didn't really enquire too much, but I know she's not into teaching art anymore. Something about starting up a ceramics studio, designing elaborate frescos & tiled floors & fittings. I got the impression she's a tad ashamed of her clientele – bound to be the fat cats & cronies building their new palaces in the hills. The flat is v. well decorated. She's invested in some fine works of local art. Hung them well too. Impressive: the eye for arrangement, the overall aestheticism of the place. I felt as if I'd entered a pleasure dome, out from the wastes of a desert.

She'd pre-cooked an Italian chicken dish, reheated it on the stove & tossed together a salad. I cracked open a bottle of Simonsvlei Pinotage, 2002. We drank & ate & in the background a CD of rustic Spanish folk music played. We talked of everything & nothing. The usual. Then she let out a measured sigh & said, 'Ian, don't you sometimes think all of this is totally unreal?'

The comment threw me somewhat. I looked at her & thought about what she meant, but words failed me.

She continued, 'I mean, this life we live here, doesn't it seem totally divorced from reality?'

I considered. 'I suppose it's unique all right. We're certainly living a life few people overseas could ever imagine.'

She sipped her wine but looked a little downcast all of a sudden, as if something was weighing down on her.

'But that's just where you're wrong,' she said. 'We're not living it are we? We're just fuckers on the sideline, bystanders, even worse than that, totally oblivious saprophytes who just plod along in our little world of perceived hardships we so selfishly claim to be our own.'

I was quite taken aback by her tone of voice. 'What do you mean?'

She sat back in the couch & gave a half smile. 'Oh I don't know. Nothing really I suppose. It just makes me wonder if we have the right to claim we're part of an experience we're actually 99 per cent removed from & untouched by, that's all.'

I thought long about this & something of a protracted silence fell between us as we finished the chicken & the bottle of wine. I knew what she meant, but somehow I didn't want to accept the biting way she put it. I've always been self-obsessed to a degree I know alienates people – it boiled down to our initial split – but I've always been content to believe that I'm at the centre of my own world & by extension that world revolves around me. To think that conception is inaccurate, that Alicia is perfectly correct in saying us whites are actually living in a fool's paradise, that we don't know an iota of what's really going on out there, left me feeling unsettled.

A little later we made love tenderly & without forewarning. I laid her out along the wide cream couch & peeled down her panties & ran an eager finger across her moistening clitoris & then rolling on a condom from my wallet I pulled my body up against hers & eased myself into her. Utter bliss.

I left late. After sex we lay together for some time, dozing on & off, I think both succumbed to some indolent mood. Then finally I whispered to her that I had best make a move. I told her the power was out & that I was apprehensive about the house being left in the dark. That may have been the truth, or it may have been an excuse to slip away from a situation that had gradually become awkward. I had noticed a subtle frigidness sidle into her body & I presume she noticed the same in me for we parted with an unstated but mutual understanding that perhaps the events of the night best be considered a random undertaking & not the start of a fresh entanglement. We were subject to all the typical post-coital indecisions & reservations I suppose.

24 November

Am deeply perturbed. After thinking yesterday was a one-off, Alicia began texting during the afternoon & by evening I was back at her place & events repeated themselves. When I left it had begun to drizzle. The windscreen had misted over & I had some problems navigating my way down the potholed roads in the dark. Large tracts of the neighbourhoods I drove through were completely black. I stopped at the intersection by the Catholic church where the traffic lights were off. I looked right & left but before I could accelerate, the oddest thing happened – a man pushing a wheelbarrow veered in front of my headlights. He stopped & put his hands up to signal my attention & then started walking towards the car.

My gut instinct was to put my foot down hard & either drive through him or else try to skirt round him. But in the panic my foot slipped on the accelerator & the car jerked forwards & stalled. By then he was at my side window, tapping vigorously. The fright I got. I didn't know what to do or think, & was only aware of the need to be compliant. I kept telling myself, 'If you antagonize this man he's going to pull out a pistol or a knife.' I inched down my window & he leered in at me.

'Please,' I began to say, 'I don't want any trouble, okay. We can talk.'

But it wasn't what I expected at all. He began to plead with me desperately, saying, 'Ah, baas, please help me, baas, please.'

Tried to smell if he was drunk or high on weed but it didn't seem so. Then I thought perhaps he was just a beggar trying his luck.

'I can't help you,' I said, waving him off, 'I don't have any money on me.'

He said, 'No, baas, I don't want money.'

'What then? What do you want?'

'My wife, she is having baby,' & he pointed to the barrow still sitting blurred & bulging in my headlights. I looked at it & registered through the stark slats of drizzle the figure of a woman lying squat on her back with her legs spread across the handlebars, clutching her swollen stomach. A most bizarre sight. V. surreal moment.

I started to do up the side window, saying, 'No no, what do you think I am, hey?' Part of me still thinking it was an ambush, a hijacking.

He said, 'Please, baas, we just need lift to clinic, please, please.'

But by then the window was up & I had started the ignition & pulled away, passing the barrow with the woman & him rushing towards her in the rain. This was all I could see of them from my rear-view mirror before they vanished almost instantly in the folds of darkness.

Drove the rest of the way home v. disturbed. Kept playing the scene over in my mind. The cold, hard, reality of it. Something grainy, pared, raw. It's late now & I'm tired. But I can't seem to get it out of my mind.

25 November
Morning

How did they proceed on in the dark after me? How did they make it with the rain falling over them like a scourge over the plagued? How did they navigate the unseen potholes? What if the wheel of that barrow got wedged in a crater in the road? What if she was thrown off? What if the man, already tired, exhausted, spent, had to heave with all his might to lift it? To deliver it from the ground? Did they make it in the end, just him, his wife & the barrow trundling those slimy hellish roads all the way to the clinic? Or did they encounter someone else, some-one with a little compassion & humanity to finally help them? How many others did he try & plead with – how often was he left crying in anguish as another car sped quickly from their midst? And after all that, what of the clinic? Did they get all the way there? If they got all the way there, she most likely being hit with labour contractions closer & closer together, what were they then confronted with? A building deserted of unpaid, striking staff? The gates shut, bolted, padlocked? What if there was no room for them there? If the beds were full of cholera victims & AIDS sufferers? What if they turned them away? What then? An unseemly birth in the first dry place they could find? Under a tree or a bus shelter or in an alleyway littered with snoozing drunks, rats, rancid garbage, excrement? Would he know what to do? Would he know to tell her to breathe at the right times, to push when needed, to hold her hand & let her squeeze it through? Should the miracle occur & the baby be born despite all this adversity, against all the odds that the cruel world has thrown at its first weak & wistful breath, will it then survive at all? Given they would have nothing dry to wrap it in & little chance they could incubate it if the rain continued to fall, as it did all night, at times in torrential gusts.

Noon

I can't exorcize it. Something beyond an image is pinned to my mind. Something about that wheelbarrow. Something about the sight of it there on the asphalt. Something about the sight of its heaped human cargo, dumped in it. So grotesque & wretched. Something about the image that furls in me, the image that makes me associate her with visions incarnate of every evil blight beset on man. Something about the weight she carries like a burden into the world. Something about the inventiveness of it too. Something startling, wonderful. To resort to such measures – such an indictment yet a testimony too. Something signalling the allotment of one man's entire desperation.

Later

Why can't I just shrug it off, internally, as I do every other savage tragedy that unfolds about me every day? Like when I'm driving & stop at intersections & tatty, filthy, balding, belly-swollen children tap at the windscreen & look at me pleadingly & cup their hands for money? Why can't I just roll the window up on this one, cut off the sound of his breathing, his pleas, as I do with all the others? Why is it my fault another tyrant in this world has chosen to cling to power? Why am I the one left now to weigh that cost?

Evening

Tell yourself you're being ridiculous. I'm being ridiculous. Any person in that position, given the times we live in, times of lawlessness, violence, crime (yes, spell it out to yourself – lawlessness, violence, crime) would have done exactly what you did. Now realize this sovereign point: it's your God-given right to protect yourself first & foremost, even your natural right to act as you did, out of precaution, out of trepidation, out of rank fear. Call it what you will. It's the nature of man, the nature of the beast in us all. Try to think of this instead: Alicia's cunt slick & wet before you, waiting to be eaten. Waiting to be parted & fucked.

26 November

Slept badly. A glumness has descended over me. My existence is banal. Moped about. Tried to read but my eyes just scanned the pages. Sat hunched at the piano, fingers dead & heavy on the keyboard. The Waldstein just seems too difficult now. I'm bored with the mistakes I make & the disjointedness of the sound I produce. Staggered for a while, around the house which is no longer mine. The gardens that belong to a holding company. All the furniture & clutter I haven't got the energy to start packing up & getting rid of. Not really sure of my existence at all today. Odd remark to record. Everything a fraction removed, my mind seems half shut to the reality of things. Did some chores. Not in the mood for Alicia today. Ignored her texts. Power still off. Going to sleep & draw a curtain over the world.

27 November
Morning

Bad dreams. Hot, restless night. Images roving at me, sounds of the fractured Waldstein. The pulverizing sight of the woman on the barrow; the man at my window; Alicia's strange pronouncements the night of the recital; the whole saga of Tobias's leg; leaving school; selling the house; the darkness. All morphed into one image. At one point thought my head was going to explode. Got up this morning & shoved four Disprin down my throat but I've got a feeling this is no ordinary headache.

Later

Thought: I've been living here, in the country of my birth, in the land of my parentage, all this time – haven't left at all – & I've experienced everything: the whole journey of a fledgling country, from birth to now, thirty years later. I was just a small boy when this country came into being. I was tiny when they signed the charter & Dad came back from the bush & put aside his fatigues & pledged allegiance to the new republic. It was a new beginning for everyone. A fresh slate. So we've been side by side, siblings in infancy, in childhood, in adolescence, as adults.

Realization: I've been a willing participant, a screw its machinery, its mechanisms. A component part to every little thing.

Question: am I to blame?

Later

The admission ought to come now that I've sunk into something of a depression. Perhaps this has been coming on for a time now & I should have seen the signs but didn't. Have just become used to how life is here, how every little stress gets notched up on the psyche & becomes the new benchmark for normality. The ever-shifting sands of sanity. I thought I had become immune to it. I thought it was branded into my mind, absorbed into my pink skin. Yet peel away the top layer & we have a nation of psychotics hankered down there in the muck. Maybe Alicia's on the verge too? Maybe we're more susceptible, us 'types'. I fear that the proverbial great wave is coming. Everyone standing in its surge.

Addendum

Going back to that previous thought – is it not too easy to surmise I am to blame because I am part of the country? Isn't it more pertinent to say the country & I are actually divorced & therefore, because of the separation, we are both to blame? To allegorize: in our parallel growths, a great divide was drawn on the day of our births. It was drawn in the sand. (In fact it was never erased from days gone before.) It was drawn there between this nation & me. A divide separating race from race, man from fellow man. In that disjointed state we have grown up deformed, autistic, simpleminded, unable to reach maturity. Or conversely, we are both fully fledged beasts, both alike in brawn & breast & brainlessness. We bash one another with the clubs of our tongues, the boots of our contempt. Or further yet, we were both stillborn & only our vengeful infant souls waft the mythic air, circling one another like weary tramps in the night. Or we are nothing at all. We were not born, in that sense of the word. We're a miscarriage of ideals. And nothing can come of us that is any good. The body has rejected us, aborted us unseemly twins. Where then is the new conception, the new birth?

1 December

In between snatches of sleep & a raft of ponderous thoughts, I slip a notepad & a blunt pencil into bed with me & I jot down ideas, observations, questions I have of myself. I write a screed of notes, scribbling sometimes out of what seems an automation, driven on by some force within me. I have to keep doing this to keep the dark fear out.

3 December

Have been writing almost constantly. Lots of it I tear up, having started a train of thought & then discarded it. Other stuff I keep prodding at, nudging the idea, the notion a little further, seeing if it will snap. Between sloth & slumber thus I levitate. Am beginning to sketch in my mind an idea of how, if anything, I can make up for that night in the rain when I failed to help that man & his wife. For I believe that's the catalyst, the genesis of my decline. Everything else is a building block towards this juncture, this point in time where I hurtle along that dark rainswept road & at that intersection, from the crossroads, there comes a man wheeling a barrow with a woman atop & an infant clawing to be born & where our paths cross something *happens*, some interconnection is formed which is fate-ordained & can't be undone.

4 December

This venture has to born out of a desperate need to come clean, to make up for my failings as a human being, as a participator in the suffering of my own kinsmen. Alicia summed it up best when she said that we – the whites – don't have the right to claim we're part of an experience we're removed almost entirely from. How can a white man in Africa ever know what it means to suffer at the hand of the oppressor when by our very lineage we are often the oppressor ourselves? Even by default, even unwittingly, even now, when we all squeal the cries of the victim, we cannot extradite ourselves from guilt. We may not be the tyrant incarnate, but we're nonetheless the silent, serpentine collaborators in a vast, encompassing crime against people on our own land, of our own soil – our fellow human beings.

There – it's said. Can I bear to look over this entry again, to look it in the face?

Later

What is the best way to pay due recompense for my role in this crime? To atone for my failure to help that man & his wife in their moment of need? What is to be my punishment? How will I suffer, as they have suffered at my hands?

Surely the only way would be for the event to occur all over again & for me to place myself at their disposal until we reach the clinic & the baby is delivered. I'd be of service to them, one man to another. But then, given that I own a vehicle & they don't, or given that I belong to the privileged & they to the peasantry, or that I am white & they are black – in short, that my *status* is one exalted over theirs – such an act would be one of charity only & while that in itself is a worthy notion, it would mean I was a willing participant, I was merely tolerating their intersection into my life, *pitying* them, & as such I would be achieving nothing. While I may be inconvenienced, I wouldn't be part of the *experience* of suffering, of hardship.

What then if that man had pulled out a pistol or a knife & hijacked me & forced me to drive him & his wife to the clinic? In that instant, surely, the roles would've reversed beyond my control & I'd have become his victim & he my aggressor & his status, given the bearing of a weapon, would exceed mine, meaning I would have no choice but to obey his every command in fear for my life. In effect, his aggression would *enslave* me. By force he'd have entered my space & taken possession of me.

And is this not the heart of the matter? Is this not what I am ultimately guilty of? Oppression, enslavement? It's the colonial blood that surges through my veins, the history that constructs me, the attitude I adopt. It has defined me all along, has made me complicit. A hundred years ago on the spot where I write this now, it is no secret at all that my forefathers enacted the heinous misdeeds that constitute human bondage, ranging about the plains with shotguns & sjamboks, coercing men to their labour by fear & oppression, demeaning them by stripping away every right a human being ought to own by birth & now, a century on, the only evident change is a physical one. We have substituted the whippings & beatings & the barrel of a gun with something equally extortionate; we have refined our methods but continue the abuse. We have substituted the loss of our status with an attitude equal to it. In short, we continue.

But returning to the man & his gun, & to my quest for punishment – it would be pointless undergoing such a brief & painless submission. I'd succumb to his threat & open the back door to let them hustle in & then drive while he pointed the knife or the gun at my neck. The fear may be punishment itself, but the hardship would be trite. A ten-minute ordeal & afterwards I'd just drive away, a little shaken, a little numb with nausea, but none the worse for wear.

No. It's no good just being a slave in the theoretical sense. I'd have to enact it too. I'd need to endure the toiling, the physical pain, the abject suffering. I'd need to withstand this over a lengthy period of time, to be brought to my knees, to be ill-treated, to be whipped if I fall behind in my labours or the ordeal overcomes me.

Moreover, to be a slave, to be punished as a slave, I'd need to be silenced. I'd need to be rendered voiceless, speechless, whether my tongue is cut from my mouth or my lips bound with a gag, so that I'd be deprived of the ability to beg, plead, reason with my master. In the same way I roll up the window on the calls of the beggars, my white ears deaf to their anguished black lips.

Later

I ponder this: is the act, *could* the act – of writing, of sitting down & chaining myself slavishly to my desk & writing page after page after page until my fingers stiffen (or even blister & bleed) & my back aches & my eyes strain & my head dizzies with tiredness be in any way an act of recompense? The discourse a form of labour; every page my servitude, its completion my liberty, the whole ordeal my catharsis?

5 December
Early morning

During the night I sketched this in my head: I have my protagonist captured & enslaved at the very beginning. Taken against his will. Tied up & shackled off. He's traded for some reason, as lowly as he is he has value to someone. Or someone needs him for something, some task a slave undertakes, carrying or hauling or digging. Perhaps carrying something on a long journey. A primitive land where everything is apocalyptic dust & ruin, in the aftermath of some war, some famine. Something to make it all the more taxing, all the more gruesome. The pain must be the thing. I want to feel it through him, every step.

Later

To add: would it not be preferable if I was another being altogether? An animal, a beast of burden perhaps, so that my master would not need to be lumbered with the prospect of feeling an iota of compassion for my suffering? It would be easier for him if he didn't. I'd have to obey his every command for fear of my life. Then I'd be a slave, punished as a slave, true to the word. I'd be at his beck & call, subject to his every whim, his every command. I'd need to live off every word he said, wait with bated breath for my next instruction. In the end I'd be so conditioned to my lot that the very notion of freedom would slip from me like a coat & I'd lose my identity, my sense of self in the raw, naked service of another.

17 December

When the notes & scraps & questions became page-long ramblings I found myself sitting up in bed & writing for hours at a time. It got uncomfortable. I migrated to my desk, installed myself one morning with a ream of newsprint I dug out of a box of school papers & a blue biro & my notebooks beside me & I've been continuing to scribble & scrawl my musings & imaginings ever since, page after page, hour upon hour, day after day. A strange compulsion. The house is in a mess. Sometimes I'm disturbed by calls & people asking to come round & look at what's for sale. They do come. They must think me odd. I haven't shaved for a week. They pick around & offer me money & I rarely think about it, just accept it. Off they trundle, parts of my existence wedged in the boots of their cars. The lounge suite already gone, the dining-room table, the garden set, lots of stuff from the kitchen. Have given up aspirations of the Waldstein. Had to when the piano was sold. Am not eating v. well. Power off. Have ignored Alicia's texts & been curt with her on the phone. She quipped something like: 'Leopards never change their spots.' Take it the whole dalliance is off. Not fazed. All is writing. My life is the desk, the paper, the pen.

5 January

Here I have remained almost ever since, in my den all hours of the day & night. My eye droops across the page, my hand scribbles on & even when the light of day fades & the night comes up, I do not put a halt to this streaming narrative. I just stagger my way into the bare kitchen & probe the windowsill & find there the shaft of a candle I light with a box of matches & carry it back to my little desk where now all this paper lies heaped in an unmitigated mess. Here I'll sit all hours of the night & not think a thing of it. But sometimes the stub of the candle goes dead & I do sneak off to bed.

7 January

I write of blood & violence & untold misery. Of hacked corpses littered on the ground, lifeless terrains & starvation. It comes to me from an imagined horror, of what could be, of the potential of human depravity. Sometimes it makes me feel sick. Sometimes I want to recoil from the page until I realize, with an equal numbing dread, that all my prophecies are real.

8 January

When I surface from the malaise of writing that I can't seem to stop, I sometimes wonder about Tobias & his poor leg. About the pain sunk there, the sore that wouldn't go away because it had, at last, after years of being held in abeyance, lingering beneath his black skin, broken through to the surface, manifested itself as a mark on him, a mark of the abuse he'd suffered. Then I think about his cries & his pleading to me. How he came to me in pain & how I fobbed him off time & time again with the white pills I tossed him, like a bone tossed to a begging dog to shut it up. It's nothing new, my crime. It stretches back to the day I could talk, to the day I learnt to utter commands from my chattering toddler tongue & realized that out of the shadows someone soon came running, a vague but eager black figure, smiling always, keen to impress, to ingratiate, to pick up the toys I left strewn across the carpet, clean the green juice I'd spilt on the floor, wipe my snotty nose, my stinking arse.

Did he get home? Did he make it there? Or was he stopped along the way & beaten & intimidated? Did militia youths pounce on him & attack him for no reason save the impunity they've been granted in their tyrant's name? His bowler hat knocked off, his little cane snapped in half. His proud checked suit torn, his knapsack snatched. I'm given to thinking the worst. I hope I'm wrong. But wherever he may be meandering, homewards to his village, or rested up there, glad to be rid of his uncaring, demanding boss for a while, if I could say anything to him, it would be: Tobias, you served me & my family for all these years uncomplainingly. What makes a man serve & yet in the end, at the final counting, not seem at all like a servant? Please share your secret.

9 January

Restless. The pace of my all-consuming pursuit has waned in the past few days. Can't think why, can't place it. Went for a sleep this afternoon. (Barely have a bed left to sleep in the rate everything is being snatched up.) Suddenly I awoke knowing a dreadful truth. I got on the phone to Veronica straight away.

'Tell me the man who bought my house isn't who I think he is?'

'Darling, what do you mean?'

'The man who bought my house – my family home – he's not, he's not one of them is he? The anonymity, the shady holding company, the cash in hand – who has access to that kind of money these days? Hey? Who's going around buying up property without even stepping foot in the place? Hey, tell me that?'

But the phone line had already gone dead.

And so it's confirmed: I am embroiled to the neck in the corruption of this place. Wedged neatly in place in a system I help feed & fatten.

10 January

I don't know how to end my story. I'm trapped, enslaved here, true as the word. I keep fearing that if I don't end my chore, if I don't see my narrative to its conclusion, then the text is going to kill me – metaphorically, psychologically – will at some point lunge out & deal the death blow. But now I see that is not going to happen. Instead it is left to me, as a final cruel irony, to kill the story. I will have to find a way. I'll have to do it sometime soon.

11 January

Why has my narrative faltered? Why has my tale come to a grinding halt? I haven't been able to write for some time now. Have not been able to resolve it, to get to the end, to a place where I can say, enough, let the child at last be born, let this painful journey be over. It was going so well. All those days it came spinning out of me in a deluge. My beast was suffering well enough. How he's laboured for the purposes of the narrative. He's tired & aching. One can't decry the need now for an end to it all, some well-earned respite. I'm exhausted sitting here. My back is killing me, my neck stiff from the poise I keep, huddled over this stack of papers all day. Why have I complicated matters, why have I let them wander from me – those boys first of all, then the pair of them driving off in a blue sedan, then the man getting himself shot, the woman disappearing – why has it all gone so awry? They were never supposed to go near that road: I knew the temptations.

If only he had had a voice from the beginning & I could have had him say: *Enough, this was a false move. My sole purpose, my sole existence even, is in the immediate service of that woman and her unborn child. Let me take a step back & undo my last few paces & put back the ropes & rebuild the cart & move with haste down the kopje & back across the veld & to the road & catch them in their folly as they try the ridiculous notion of attempting to drive a car off into the unseen distances where utter doom is their only fate! 'Wait for me,'* he'd call out. *'I'll keep walking for you, I'll do what I can.'*

12 January

No one to blame but myself. Terrible night. Giddy with thoughts that kept coming to me, over & over. Finally arrived at a horrid, pertinent truth.

Out there my donkey stands beside a gunned-down sedan, while somewhere, breezing along the firmament, hovers my authorial hand of God, the ultimate hand of fate. I should have been able to stop that lot disappearing one by one from my narrative. A writer is supposed to be the most omnipotent god-voice in existence: I'm supposed to be in charge & my characters are supposed to obey me. Why have they deserted me like this, fled me just before the grand climax?

This is what I now believe: I have come to suspect that they have acted in unison against me. I truly thought that by undertaking this mammoth task, subjecting myself to the pain of this cognitive exercise, I was atoning for my failure to act that night, or on any other occasion, or for being nothing more than a passive bystander in the collapse of a system, rather than share my load, pay my dues. I thought I was stepping inside the experience. I perceived my metamorphosis, my reduction to the most lowly of beasts, to be an act of homage to those people, an offering. But now I see I have done nothing but re-enact my crime. I have done it again. I kick them when they are down, writhing on the road, & I put a boot into their backs.

I – the donkey – we – were never their slaves. Paradoxically, by the mere fact that I controlled their every move, their every facet of being, by the instance that I plucked them out of my imaginings & held them forcibly in this narrative, I enslaved *them*. As author I am *their* master, they my slaves. I have been controlling their destiny, their fate was in my hands; just as it was that night when our paths crossed at that intersection & in my position of omnipotence – by the mere designation of my status as someone who had the cards in his hand, who could *choose* a path of action & not be subjected to it – I became the author of that man & his wife's destiny. I *enslaved* them to my choice.

217

Is it any wonder that the subconscious realization of this caused the fracturing of the story? Is it any wonder they conspired to break free from me, *their* master, just as my beast had longed to break free from them? It is any wonder when they were nothing more than stereotypes from the beginning, picked to represent a principle in motion as opposed to the reality of the human experience?

Even their hellish post-war surroundings I merely gleaned from my memory, from international newsfeeds documenting the blight of the warlord across Africa, the genocides, the massacres, the ethnic cleansing. It was a landscape pre-painted for me, a template of numerous composites. And the descriptions of the wild they trod across? Who would know that I sit here at my pine desk & lying beside me are a series of reference books which I plunder with regularity? *The Bundu Book 1: Trees, Flowers and Grasses of the Veld. The Bundu Book 2: Geology, Gemmology and Archaeology.* For the truth is I haven't been into the heart of the country for some time. I haven't experienced it.

I sit here in shame. Perhaps it's from this understanding I know I need to leave. That I can never be reconciled to this place. Maybe I have found my reason.

13 January

I think about them in this vein a lot now. I know I haven't done them justice, given them a real voice, made them real human beings. I didn't see them beyond significations of what they stood for & hence they never stood a chance. In this admission alone I find the entire weight of my failure come down on me. I had never stopped to think what tribe they belonged to, what their origins were, their genesis, of which chiefdom they called themselves. And where is the kraal that is their motherland? Take the boys. I perceived them to be well conditioned. Their physiques are of men of the land. True men, in any sense, in any culture. Dare I imagine their communion with the hoe & the budza & the panga from an early age? Each bundled tight to his mother's back (whoever she may be) & she all day in the fields labouring in the full scorn of the sun. Those lean black chests bare to the elements all boyhood, splicing wood, ploughing troughs, clubbing samp, in ways that would be their daily ceremonial.

All I chose to depict of the woman was her condition. I chose to make her the product of her pain & discomfort. The continual sourness of her character. But what I failed to do is look beyond type, look at the person, the race she is descended from. Had I done this I would have realized my gross misrepresentation. Isn't it well known in their myths that the mother-to-be labours on undeterred & when the time comes she drops the hoe in the field & births there astride it & is handed the hoe again when the grisly umbilical cord is snipped (yes indeed – snipped – with that same blade that breaks the soil!).

I suspect I've made too much of her complaining, her weakness, understandable as it is. If the journey was to take place again tomorrow, if I were to wake up & take to my desk & everything were to fracture around me (& if he were to saunter off from the plantation & by some miracle find a patch of vegetables & there be captured), I'm convinced the woman, in light of my new reflections, would be a far tougher, far more co-operative soul. Perhaps then our paths would never need to cross & that's as it should be?

Later

I'm disheartened that I can't do more for them. But maybe I can. Maybe the least I can do is finally give them names, baptize them in my mind? Knowing them as well as I do, I expect I should. So enough of 'the man' & 'the woman' & 'the boys' as if they're just Everyman pieces in a medieval miracle play. The man I think I'll call Baba. Baba – father. It's obvious I'll call the woman Amai. Amai – mother. What to call the two boys? How about: the one Farai, the other Kudzai?

14 January

Perhaps, in my mind, at least I feel as if I've set them free. Even in death – if I can't resurrect Baba, Farai & Kudzai – if, in some way, their deaths are a sacrifice for the greater good, then perhaps they are free on their own terms. Free from my tyranny. Up there in the spirit world, or cast adrift on a crisp white piece of paper, a kind of heaven for dead characters. I don't have time to indulge in this any more. Not now, anyway.

The lady from Auction Express arrived today & behind her a huge lorry. Away went the last of my life. Talk about leaving it late. All I have now is a suitcase, a few shackles, few books. They took my desk from under me, almost. I had to lift the cluster of papers, & this journal, as they carted it away from where I sat. So much to do.

Even as ruthless as I've been in stripping away my life of late, I haven't been entirely successful. Can one ever be? Have heaps of boxes sitting around filled with bric-a-brac that I don't know what to do with. Amazing the junk one can acquire in a lifetime. The baggage of one's existence. Piles & piles of stuff I've turfed out to Sixpence. Must think Christmas has come all over again. He brims from ear to ear & goes off down to his kia laden with boxes & packets & bundles. Later on I'll square up with him as there won't be time tomorrow morning before I leave. (Intend to get away at six on the dot: optimistic?) He's staying on & in many ways I'm relieved about that. I'll look him squarely in the eye – well I intend to – & say, 'Sixpence, look after the garden, hey – nice, nice.'

The house is empty & in every room there is an echo that trails after you. Feels like a sad lament, as if it's mourning my departure already. Ridiculous assumption. But how many months will she stand empty, stocking up value but losing the essence of a home? Something deep down tells me all this has been a colossal fuck up. Yet I suppose last-minute reservations are not an uncommon affliction.

I have not spoken to Mom & Dad for some months now. Doubtless they tried to phone at Christmas only to find the line dead, disconnected weeks ago. Alex & James may have sent e-mails. I guess I'll find out when I reach South Africa & plug in a cable to reconnect with reality.

I'll be sleeping in a sleeping bag on the floor tonight. Not looking forward to it. Anticipate I'll be stiff as hell tomorrow & rue the decision, the whole trip to the border. I could have gone to stay with friends. People have offered. Linda & Ron for one. I played with the idea of sneaking back to Alicia's, one last night, one last romp. Not that I think she'd have me now. I don't think I'm fickle with other people's emotions but I keep my distance. I don't know why. I read & I suspect someday a book will tell me. Books & writing have been my anchor.

Muss es sein? Es muss sein.

Later

Shuffled everything into the few boxes that will fit into the car, rolled out the petrol containers. One I funnelled into the tank, the other I'll need about an hour before the border if everything goes according to plan. Have checked passport, car documents. Have a flask of water, some packets of crisps.

Now what? Deathly hollowness in the house. I'm sitting on the floor in the study, my sleeping bag next to me. It's a hot night. Turns out there is about half a candle left. The power will never come back, I believe. Not real power. When the candles across the city & then further across the country all finally burn into noth-ingness, & the paraffin stocks for the hurricane lamps dry up, is this the point when darkness will finally come forever to these people? When the anarchy will at last break & 'be loosed upon the earth'?

Is there no way to avert this? Is there no way the story can end, the child can be born of a new generation, free from the seeds of the past?

What if we – my donkey & I – embark upon a journey, a long journey to an unspecified destination, far away? What if we begin it tomorrow? We will be trotting along, or driving along quite pleasantly, having shed our burdens & the ropes that bound us one way or another. It'll be a hot, cloudless day. Then ahead we'll see, perhaps round a bend, a car parked on the side of the road, a blue car, a small sedan. We'll see this car & at first our instincts won't be particularly aroused because there isn't any-thing uncommon about a car stationed by the roadside. So we'll think nothing of it, nothing, that is until we are almost along-side it. Then we'll see something which piques our attention. Nothing immediately alarming, nothing that shudders through the brain. Yet at once we'll sense a certain neediness emanating from the figure who stands beside it clutching her stomach. A certain look of distress, or discomfort. Enough to make us feel that we have a duty to stop & reverse, or turn around, & offer our assistance.

We'll pull up alongside this woman – we won't even register the colour of her skin – & see with shock the state of her condition, the urgency of her need. In a language all three of us will understand, whether it be English, or a traditional language or even the silent transferral of meaning between man & beast, between beings of different yet equal distinctions, we will say, 'Are you okay? Do you need our assistance?'

At this point she'll look up, hardly aware, because of her distress, that we have come to aid her, & she'll smile & we'll see relief & gratitude break over her face & flush away the panic that held her, the panic of being out here alone with a baby on the way.

With that smile she'll say, 'Oh thank you, thank you, how I've been waiting for someone to stop & help.'

She may break away in a convulsion of pain, a labour contraction & we who are not so familiar with the inflictions of childbirth will panic, perhaps even more than she, & without hesitation we will be jolted into action.

We'll take her underarm & support her to the car, or perhaps we'll even crouch down low on the ground & she'll ease herself onto our back & grip our neck or our ears & we'll rise gently & go staggering off. We'll make haste, trotting if we can, or streaming along the roads at great speeds & we'll keep telling her that it's all going to be fine, that we'll make it in time. We'll say, 'Don't worry, amai,' or, 'Don't worry, mother, it won't be long.' She'll be breathing deeply now, the contractions coming closer, the pain intensifying. But at least she'll know she's in good hands. She'll lie there & know she doesn't have to worry because in the end her fears were appeased, someone has stopped, someone has given her a helping hand.

Speeding along as quickly as we know how, our charge clinging on behind, we'll finally see a sign ahead, just left off the road, a rickety silver-sheeted sign posted into the soil with a slender white cross painted on. Streaking behind it is a sandy slip of a road which we'll turn down & hurry along, kicking up dust in our path. The road straightens & will lead us to a low fence where there's there a plough-disc with the same white cross. The gates will be open. We'll see a water tank on stilts & around a wisp of bush there'll be a modest clutch of buildings. We'll race up & stop & at once there'll be three nurses who come rushing out to meet us. They'll be wearing pale blue uniforms with crisp white wimples. We'll be relieved to see them, women who know what to do in these circumstances.

They will aid her out of the car & she'll hobble in their clutch & just before she disappears into the ambient coolness of the wards she will look back & say, or mouth, in the language which is universal to us all, 'Thank you.'

There will be nothing more we can do. We won't know what happens. We won't know how long it will be until that baby is delivered. Until it is brought into this world, until its first screams break out over the labour ward & one of the nurses bundles it in swaddling & lays it close to the bosom of its mother.

There'll be nothing more we can do but we'll have done enough. We will leave, driving away or walking on in the sun. We'll go on with our lives.

It's late. Better stop. Long day ahead tomorrow. It's hard to fathom that in two days I start at the new school. There is only a tiny flicker of the candle left. It dances in the last pool of wax, the last thread of string it clings to. I'm going to stop writing now & when I put the last full stop on the page I'm going to shut this journal & wait a moment & then blow the candle out.

Acknowledgements

I am indebted to a reading of Michel Foucault's essay, 'Qu'est-ce que l'auteur?', translated from the French by Jouse V. Harari, in *Textual Strategies: Perspectives in Post-Structuralist Criticism,* edited by J. Harari, pp. 141–160 (Methuen & Co. Ltd).

I am extremely grateful to Mrs Drue Heinz for providing me with a residential Hawthornden Fellowship in May 2009 which allowed me to complete work on a draft of this novel.

I am likewise grateful to my editor, Francesca Main, and publisher, Suzanne Baboneau, at Simon & Schuster, and to my agent, Bruce Hunter, at David Higham Associates.